# Scar Tissue

**David Skivington**

Scar Tissue
Copyright © David Skivington 2013
ISBN 978-1-906377-68-7

Fisher King Publishing Ltd
The Studio
Arthington Lane
Pool-in-Wharfedale
LS21 1JZ
England

Cover Photo by Susan Aurinko

For my amazing wife Bee.

Without you it would

not have been possible.

# Acknowledgements

First of all I would like to thank God for putting so many amazing people in my life, although there are too many to mention here by name.

Thank you to my wonderful family. You have always been there and supported me through many crazy ideas, giving wisdom and love.

Thanks to Robert Henshilwood, Reuben Hollebon and Tom Pateman for taking the time to sit and read the first drafts and giving your insight to help improve the novel. Also to Malcolm Egner of Dalit Freedom Network, who was able to give stories, facts and figures to help make sure that the novel was as realistic as possible. Kimberely Rae (author of *Stolen Woman*) and Daniel Walker (author of *God in a Brothel* and Executive Director of Nvader charity), thank you for sharing your knowledge on human trafficking and your contributions and suggestions.

To the Wednesday Night group, for all your encouragement and prayers, especially Nick and Linda Castle and Matt and Hannah Read. You have taught me to keep dreaming and never to give up. To Chris St Claire Whicker who always makes me strive for better in my writing and from life.

A big thank you also to Charlotte Miller for your introductions. Also to Rick at Fisher King Publishing for seeing the potential in the novel and Sam for her patience with all the changes I kept making!

Grateful thanks to Susan Aurinko for the front cover image, who knew our chance meeting in Jaipur would be so fruitful!

I would like to say a massive thank you to my beautiful, talented and very lovely wife Bee. You have been with me through all of it, encouraging and critiquing, helping me to keep going when the end seemed a long way off.

Finally I would like to say thank you to you, the reader. I hope you enjoy the novel, and if you feel challenged about the issue of human trafficking or the treatment of the Dalits please take a few minutes to look at the list of charities, at the back of the book, doing amazing work to fight these injustices.

# Chapter One

The smell of incense hung sickly sweet in the air, but it was too rich, too strong: a poor attempt to cover the aroma of decay which filled the room. Every breath became more constricted as the heat intensified, sapping the little of my strength which remained. My temples throbbed and the incessant blaring of car horns from the traffic outside did nothing to soothe them. I gripped the gnarled wooden table behind me for support, closing my eyes as I tried to blow the palpable stench of death from my nostrils.

"It can't be Tom: Just a mistake. Can't be Tom: Just a mistake. Can't be Tom: Just a mistake." These few words had become my mantra in the last twenty two hours. They were the only thing helping to focus my senses and stop me losing the small feeling of control I so desperately clung to, like a piece of floating debris in the ocean without which I would drown.

This insanity had begun when I was woken on Tuesday morning, the telephone's shrill cry rising to crescendo until I answered. A crackly line had greeted me in the darkness, but all that I could hear was static.

Sitting up, I ran a hand through my tangled hair then breathed in deeply, allowing the breath to leave in a steady flow. I hung up the phone and rolled over, checking the time. The neon display proclaimed it was two am. Sighing, I lay back down. But as soon as I had nestled my head into the pillow the phone screeched once more, like an alarm refusing to be ignored. I stretched out an arm from the comfort of my duvet and snatched up the receiver.

"Mrs Parker?" croaked a tinny voice with a heavy accent that I struggled to place in my sleepy state.

"Hmm?" I blearily answered, yawning as I spoke.

"Mrs Par..." The voice stopped as the line fell dead. I held the receiver in my hand for a moment, listening to the buzz while trying to gather my senses in the darkness.

As I considered the possible reasons of a call at such an hour I suddenly became alert. It had to be serious for such an early disturbance. I switched on the bedside lamp and anxiously stared at the phone, wondering what ominous tidings I was to receive. After a few seconds the phone rang again. This time I snatched it up before a full ring was uttered, my wits heightened with adrenalin.

"Mrs Par..." the voice began again.

"Who is this?" I asked, cradling the phone to my ear with both hands.

"Mrs Parker?" The voice croaked again.

"Yes, it's Mrs Parker. Who is this? What do you want?"

"It is some problem we are seeing with your husband," the

voice slowly explained, sounding irritated at having to divulge this information.

"Tom? What is it? What's he done?" I asked through the static. A deep sigh followed and then the sound of stubble rubbing against the receiver.

"I'm afraid I am calling at you for very bad reasons."

I closed my eyes and held my breath. A faint sweat appeared on my brow as numerous possibilities began to swarm in my mind.

"What do you mean for very bad reasons? Who are you and where is my husband?" I asked, my voice trembling as I tried to hide my fear. Down the receiver was the sound of a cigarette being laboriously sucked, then exhaled. It took every ounce of restraint not to scream down the phone.

"I am Chief Superintendent Roy with the Kolkata Police calling you from India Ma'am. The reason I am calling is with this very bad news."

"Kolkata? India? What? You... there must be some mistake. My husband has never even been to India! That's what has happened. It must be the wrong Mrs Parker," I said, trying to laugh at the absurdity of the situation and regain composure, but my laugh was far too high pitched to deliver the reassurance I sought, producing a squeak in the silence left by Roy as he paused to take another drag of his cigarette. His lips smacked together. I winced at the sound.

"Just a mistake," I said again quickly, to fill the silence as I absently smoothed the empty space on the bed next to me.

"I'm afraid that there is being no mistake Mrs Parker. Your husband is here with us," he said with finality.

"With you? In India? No, this doesn't make sense. He's in Newcastle at a business conference. He'll be back this afternoon. You've got it all wrong. He can clear all this up as soon as he is home," I reasoned.

Another drag. The sound of smoke blowing out again as he exhaled excruciatingly slowly. "He is most definitely here with us."

"He's in Newcastle, not India" I retorted, trying to match his assured tone.

"You are not correct Mrs Parker. I am most sure that it is him we have with us."

"Well put him on the phone then!" I demanded, clenching my fists as the sound of stubble being scratched tickled my ear.

"No, that is most definitely not possible."

"Why not? If you have him there, let me speak to him," I demanded, fear fuelling my irritation.

"Mrs Parker?"

"Stop calling me Mrs Parker and put my husband on the phone!" I screeched.

"But you see, that is the reason for which we are calling.

He cannot come and be speaking on the phone. You see, he is expired."

"What do you mean expired?"

"Dead."

Thirty six hours later I was in a dingy, sweltering, cockroach infested basement in Kolkata not much bigger than my garage. The roof was only a foot or so higher than me and halfway up each of the walls were stained with water marks. There was writing scribbled in large red letters on one wall in some sort of language but I had no idea as to its message. All that the room contained was Superintendent Roy, me, a small wooden table with matching chair, and a metal table supporting a covered body. The corpse was shrouded by a white cloth with smatterings of dried blood on it.

Despite the suffocating heat there was no fan or cooling system which left the air stagnant and rank. I feared the state of decay of the body in this humidity, just the thought of what I was to see turned my stomach. I had never before seen death so raw. It was always in a sanitised way, removed, with the body neatly wrapped, washed and hidden away in a grandly designed coffin viewed from a distance. But this was so different. Death sat on a table a few feet from me, its face soon to be exposed. What would I do if it was actually Tom? I had no idea, my heart quickening as I tried to rationalise the thought away. It was too much to comprehend.

I looked up and saw Roy staring at me as he dragged heavily on his cigarette, the ash burning right into the filter. Despite the stifling heat he was still wearing a white vest which peeked from behind his crumpled brown shirt, on which the top two buttons were missing. He tossed the cigarette stub onto the filthy concrete floor and crushed it under the heel of his boot, sending a cockroach scuttling for safety. His leisurely exhaling was the only sound in the dismal room as he stood for a moment, took a handkerchief from his pocket and wiped away the sweat which had glistened on his brow. Clearing his throat he then paced slowly across the floor, dust rising with each step and clinging to his brown uniform.

He paused for a moment behind the body and my eyes dropped to the place they had been ardently trying to avoid. Unable to look away, all I could do was repeat the mantra, "it can't be Tom, just a mistake. It can't be Tom, just a mistake," as I wrung my hands together frantically trying to stop myself from shaking. The terrifying uncertainty I had faced over the last twenty two hours was about to end but I did not know how I would cope with the possible sight that I was to be shown. Roy nodded courteously to me then pulled back the cloth as if revealing a grotesque new scientific discovery. "It can't be Tom, just a..."

A gasp escaped my cracked lips and I stumbled backwards, doubled over, gripping my stomach as if I had been kicked hard. I vomited. Then again. My breath came in short, sharp bursts as I shook my head, willing it to be untrue. Wailing, I slumped dejected onto the concrete, clutching at my hair in desperation. It took a moment for the tears to come, then they flowed, wetting my cheeks with fury as I lost all control, banging my fists on the floor as the small debris of hope swept away leaving me drowning in a vast ocean of despair.

I have no idea how long I remained on the floor. It could have been minutes, hours or days; time was an irrelevance. I had exhausted myself weeping till nothing remained but a dark emptiness as I just lay still, the image of Tom's pale, dead face hovering in front of me.

In my blackness I slowly became aware of a hand on my shoulder trying to uncurl me from the foetal position I had assumed on the grimy floor. I opened my now swollen eyes, my face awash with salty tears and dust.

"Mrs Parker. Take. Please." Roy was holding out a silver cup from which steam rose, motioning for me to take it from him. "Drink now. For your strength." He squatted next to me, placing the cup in my hands which I numbly accepted. It was too hot to hold comfortably, but the heat felt good. It seemed to replenish some sort of feeling. I wiped my eyes with my sleeve and then allowed myself to be lifted to my feet.

"Please. Drink," he instructed once more.

I robotically followed his directions, the sweetness bringing me slowly back to reality.

"Who, what…" I stammered, trying to formulate questions but failing, my mind overwhelmed with grief and uncertainty. Why was he here? Who had done this? How did he get here? "How did he die?" I finally whispered.

In response, Roy took the bloodied cloth in his hand and gently tugged it down so it sat at Tom's waist. My answer lay right there before me. In the middle of his chest it was possible to see where a bullet must have exited his flesh, taking his life. The urge to vomit fought with me once more, but this time was beaten back.

In my trance like state I gently lay my shaking hand on Tom's chest, the chill of his clammy body taking me by surprise. Instinctively I drew my hand back, then tentatively lay it once more. Nearly every part of me wanted to pull away as if, by doing so, it would not be true. It was as if I had to put as much distance between me and this incomprehensible picture as possible. Yet part of me wanted to linger. I needed to see this with my own eyes, for my heart to believe what was actually happening. Being there, in that warm, confined space, inches from the body of my recently deceased husband somehow brought a feeling of finality, helping me to begin to process all that I had discovered and to slowly grasp the reality of a nightmare. Seeing him like that felt like throwing salt on a wound. There was immediate intense pain that burned deep inside. I could see him physically in front of me, but the realisation that he would never again be by my side assaulted my consciousness.

I traced my finger around the charred flesh of the exit wound, the skin blackened and burnt. His dried blood was crusted around the edges, parts of it flaking as I touched them. I spread out each of my fingers, holding the open palm over the wound to cover it. This way I was able to see him whole again, wishing it was that easy to change everything and bring him back. To erase all that had happened and to stop this agony.

How could someone have done this to my beautiful man? What possible motive could they have had to wish him harm? My gentle, loving husband. My joy. My all.

But among these thoughts one question formed and reformed itself in my mind, growing louder and louder, needing to be heard. It was Roy who brought that question into the open.

"Mrs Parker. What do you know about your husband?"

If I had been asked that question yesterday I would have told you every fact you had wanted to know. He worked in a mid-sized insurance company. Had a salary of thirty nine thousand with hopes of promotion in the next few years. Free time spent playing football, rowing or in the gym. A hankering for blue cheese. Enjoys being tickled between the shoulder blades. Hates cats except tabbies. Self-conscious about the mole on his left ear lobe. Finds Fosters just a little too gassy. Prefers real ale by an open fire.

Any number of peculiar details I could have given in an instant. His hopes, dreams, ambitions; all shared in moments of intimacy. But now, as he lay here before me, I consider the question again. How much did I actually know about my husband? I could think of no conceivable explanation for his presence here. It was a complete mystery.

His body with its familiar curves, scars and tattoos had always felt like home. Now though, as I look at it and search for answers I feel a sense of distance. What is the reality behind them? Each part of what made him physically distinctive, made him *mine*, I now feel as if I'm looking at him for the first time. They look back at me, strange, distant, now a possible clue as to his real existence. What was once a map of home now seems a plan to a foreign, unknown terrain.

My hand rubs gently over his skin, stopping to trace the outline of an eagle's beak peering over his left shoulder. I let my hand caress it, nostalgically thinking back to the day we first met.

It was just over five years ago. Christmas was still well over a month away but approached with aggression in every shop window in the form of robotic Santas, clutches of mistletoe and the wailing voice of Maria Carey. It was already dark outside and I was curled up on a bean bag in the corner of my favourite coffee shop, tattered book in hand. The room was dingy with an orange glow, Moroccan carpets on the wall and impressive teapots full of mint tea, looking as if all they needed was a quick rub to release a genie. It was almost five and the shop was empty except for me and a dark haired, rugged looking waiter I recognised from previous trips. I was completely immersed in my reading when suddenly I heard a gruff cough. I looked up into his sparkling green eyes for the first time, not knowing I would soon wake up to them every day.

"Mind if I join you down there on those bean bags? It's just..." he looked around the empty café for emphasis, "it's not like I'm rushed off my feet. Be nice to have some company."

"Em, well yeah, I was just, yeah, please do," I stuttered. I could feel my cheeks redden as I brushed back my hair. I had been so lost in thought that I hadn't noticed him walk across from the bar and perch on a stool opposite me.

"It's Rachel, right?" he said as he clambered onto the beanbag next to me, his leg brushing mine.

"How do you know my name?" I asked defensively.

"I know more about you than you think," he said, his eyes dancing playfully at my horrified expression. "Let me see, you live at 14 Appleyard Court, you travelled here by bus today and you used to have what can only be described as a horrendous fringe!" I tried to reply, my face deepening in its scarlet colouring.

"How, who are you?"

He laughed heartily, tossing my purse into my lap. "Relax! You left your purse on the counter. The bus ticket was in there, as was your rather fetching student card avec fringe!" He smiled at me, clearly expecting it to be returned. Instead I glared at him and snatched up my purse, feeling foolish for getting over defensive and making myself look even more ridiculous in the process.

"Wow! Easy lady! Look I'm sorry, can we start over. I'm Tom," he said extending his hand in a mockingly serious way. "I've just started working here, between jobs, you know. I didn't mean to upset you. It's just, well, I spotted your purse on the counter and thought," his voice dropped to a mumble, "it would give me a reason to come and speak to you." It was his turn now to look embarrassed as he ran his fingers through his hair and looked bashfully at the ground.

"Oh, and why did you want to come and speak to me?" I asked, trying to remain haughty.

"Just because," he said looking back at me, "I thought it

would be rude to throw you out without speaking to you first. It's nearly five and some of us have got homes to go to you know!" He flashed me another cheeky grin and this time I smiled back.

"Well then, don't let me keep you, I shall be on my way this instant!" I said, standing as if to leave.

"Well, on you go, and don't forget your purse this time. Unless you fancy some food? I have some left over chocolate cake in the fridge and unless you help me I'm going to have to eat it all myself."

"Well, if I would be saving you from that, I might just see what I can do!"

"Excellent!" he said, walking towards the door and turning the sign to closed. "Ever had a lock in at a coffee shop? It's far tastier with less of a headache in the morning."

"I believe this is my first," I giggled.

"Well, I feel privileged to be here with you at this historic moment!" he said, pulling the biggest chocolate cake I had ever seen from the fridge.

"Choose your weapon," he said, laying a fork, teaspoon, table spoon and ladle on the table.

"Definitely the ladle!" I said laughing, before eyeing him suspiciously. "Do you do this for all the ladies?"

"Only the pretty ones. You're the fifth I've tried it on today and the only one foolish enough to join me."

I playfully slapped his arm.

"Kidding, just kidding! I've seen you a couple of times in the last few weeks since I started working here and I assumed anyone drinking as much hot chocolate as you must have a sweet tooth!"

"Just how long were you watching me today? I'm feeling slightly scared by your observations!"

"Let's just say long enough to see you picking your nose earlier," he said, trying to stop his lip curling into a smile.

"What! I don't, you're lying!" I said, slapping him again on the arm.

"Just joking. My observations 'ave been as followz," he said, trying to put on a nasal French accent and doing a terrible job. "You have recently finished as a student and are either unemployed, something artistic or a shift worker guessing by your timings of entry to the café. Your nails are a little long to be anything too practical, but you seem to have enough cash not to worry about treating yourself to more than the odd cuppa, so I would guess you're not unemployed, but you probably work in something irregular but rewarding as you look more content than most people in here." He tapped his teeth with his fork. "I'm going to guess, mmm, either a painter or a lion tamer?"

"Very close. I'm a photographer but dabble with lion taming in my spare time! Change that to struggling photographer, but a content one if you're to be listened to. Good detective work. Any more?" I urged, leaning closer.

"Looking at your fingers," he said as he took them in his cracked hands and caressed them gently, "I can see a definite lack of anything pretty and sparkly and you seem far too keen to speak to a dashingly handsome waiter, so I guess you're single?" he asked, raising an eyebrow.

"Keep this up and you'll have Sherlock Holmes out of a job," I said as my hand lingered in his.

"And by the fact that you are normally always the last to leave here, you probably don't have anywhere to go this evening and would love to join me for dinner?" he said mischievously.

"That's very forward!" I replied, removing my hand from his and subconsciously holding it to my chest.

"Well, if you like we could always go for a drink first if that's any less forward? I even promise to pay for at least the first round." I looked at him for a moment trying to rationally consider if this was a wise move, but already I was drunk on his charm.

"Alright, but just to stop you from stalking me!"

"Now where's the fun in that?" he retorted, taking a small step towards me.

"Seeing as you know so much about me, what do I need to know about you?" I asked, tilting my head to observe him better.

"Not much to know," he said shrugging. "With me, what you see is what you get; tall dark and handsome. Moved here a few months ago, just got the job here while I'm looking for something better. That's it, nothing more to know," he said, with a note of finality.

"Well, what brought you here? Where are you from?" I probed.

"Just around," he said vaguely, waving his hand. "I've been travelling for the last few years, but I'm here now, for a while at least."

"Glad to hear it," I said, smiling coyly at him. "What are you looking to do, for a job I mean?"

"This feels more like an interview! I can write you up a CV if you want?" He folded his arms and perched on the counter.

"I'm sorry, just curious," I began.

"A lot of dead cats could say the same thing," he said, jokingly wagging a finger at me. "Done a bit of this, bit of that, hopefully get something in business. Happy? Anything else which you have a burning desire to know?" he asked while raising his eyebrows impatiently.

"Mmm. Any previous marriages?"

"Nope." He rubbed his earlobe then leaned back, taking a spoonful of chocolate cake. "This is really good you know, you should try some," he said, waving a piece in my direction. I leant in and took a bite, nodding in agreement as the sugary goodness filled my mouth.

"Don't think you can distract me from my interrogations with your wonderful chocolate cake," I said, covering my mouth to avoid spraying him with crumbs. "Where were we? Ah, any psychotic ex-girlfriends?" I pressed.

"None to worry about. Depends on your definition of psychotic. Definitely none as nosey as you though." He smirked as I raised my eyebrows in mock offence.

"I shall ignore that. What else do I need to know? Hmm, have you any debts of over half a million?"

"Is this some sort of vetting? Look, you can just say no to the dinner if you want rather than making me sweat."

"It's more fun to watch you sweat. Any pets?" I continued.

"Nope. Most of them make me sneeze" he said half apologetically.

"Any tattoos?" He hesitated, and then rubbed his left shoulder absently.

"Just the one," he said, but as he spoke I noticed the good humoured sparkle disappear from his eye for just a second and hardness replaced it, then as quickly as it had arrived it was gone. "You're just trying to get me naked," he said, and flashed me a smile, the glint returning.

"Oh, and whereabouts would said tattoo be?" I asked

inquisitively. In a flash his shirt was off onto one of the tables, revealing a muscular torso, pitted with numerous scars. He turned his back revealing a garish drawing of an eagle in mid-flight holding a snake in one of its claws over his left shoulder. I couldn't help but laugh out loud.

"A man of artistic taste, there's my detective work."

Instantly I realised I had offended him and had been too quick to criticise. "Sorry. I didn't mean to be rude, it's just I wouldn't expect you to have a tattoo like that. You don't look the sort who..." I began, then quickly stopped as my explanation seemed to be making things even worse.

"Who would what?" he asked, through gritted teeth as he placed the shirt over his shoulder.

"It's just a bit, well, you would expect it on an old man on his motorbike, know what I mean?"

"It's my family's crest," he said, staring at me sternly, looking insulted.

"Oh, I'm sorry, it's just..." I began, completely flustered.

He laughed out loud at my discomfort. "Only kidding. It's an awful tattoo. I got it when I was younger and have regretted it ever since. Wish that I could just wash it off but sadly it's not that simple."

"What would make you get such a tattoo? Did no one tell you how bad it looked?" I asked, relieved I had not soured our initial flirting with my big mouth.

"It's a long story. In short, me and a few mates had too much to drink one night and I was dared to get it, and hey presto, ten years later it's still not magically vanished." He looked over his shoulder with distain, a grimace on his face.

"And what about this scar?" I asked, stepping closer to him and placing my hand on his chest.

"That has a very interesting story, which I would love to tell you later."

"Why later?" I whispered.

"Because I'm too busy at the moment doing this," he said, running a hand through my hair and gently leaning to kiss me.

"I can wait to hear it," I said, and leaned in, kissing him back.

# Chapter Two

*Dear Rachel,*

*Everything I have told you is untrue.*

*Our relationship was constructed on quicksand of lies which I knew would one day pull me under, and it appears, for better or worse, that time is now. The one thing I need you to hold on to as you read these next pages is that I love you. I honestly do. I don't ask your forgiveness, that would be too much after the enormous depth of deceit over such a long time, but what I do ask is that you try to understand why I have kept these things from you.*

*I am writing this letter as my way of atonement for what has happened and to reveal who I really am. I fear that if I were to do it in person the words would escape me and I would never be able to make you understand why I have done all that I have. There's so many things that I have wanted to share with you, things that have almost consumed me, but after the first few lies it became easier to hold you at a distance and present to you the reality I wanted you to see. The reality I desperately wanted to be true.*

*If only we could have met many years earlier, in a time when things were simple and I could have been the right man for you. The man worthy of your trust, your affection, your love. But when you came to me I was no longer that man.*

*Broken by life, you still loved me for the pieces that remained, seeing beyond the sharp, brittle exterior and trying to join them together to imagine me as something complete, something with value, something beautiful. It was an impossible task, but I love you for trying and I'm so sorry for failing you again and again. Time after time I lied and yet you still looked for the good in me, even when there was none.*

*How you will judge me for what I have done and what I intend to do I have no idea, but you must be told every dark secret. I will keep nothing hidden.*

*The best place to start is our first meeting. I say first meeting but I had seen you many times before. I had watched you sitting in the cafe, looking without a care in the world, totally absorbed in your book, transported to your own world of splendid isolation, content and complete. I saw you and if I'm honest I felt jealous. The beauty of being able to be so lost in that moment, free from all the concerns and worries of the past and future. I saw that in you and I wanted it, craved it for myself. Your face was so serene like that of an angel and I felt that if somehow I could make you mine that contentment would become mine too, passing as if by osmosis simply from being near you. From that moment, I knew that I needed you in my life, but was too selfish to show you who I really was so you could decide for yourself if you wanted me. Instead, I became like a chameleon, being what I felt you wanted me to be so that you would love me, keeping my actual past well hidden.*

*In our first conversation you asked me a simple question to which I created a simple lie. But the truth to that question begins to cut to the heart of my mess. I remember you asking if I had any tattoos, and I fashioned some sort of story about it being a bad mistake with friends when I was drunk. The truth is it was the most sober I have ever been. The tattoo was designed with a single purpose. It was symbolic of my entry into the loyalty of Saiful Das and his gang in Kolkata. A gang specialising in trafficking children into prostitution.*

## Chapter Three

"Mrs Parker? I am sorry to be pressing you, but as you can understand there are some details of which we need to be knowing about your husband due to the way in which he... ahh..." Roy tailed off, waving his cigarette vaguely in the air.

"Was killed?" I replied icily, finishing his sentence.

"Yes." Roy broke eye contact for a second then looked back at me. I sighed heavily, my mind teeming with thoughts as my hand continued to rest on Tom's shoulder. It almost felt as if the longer I could remain there with his body, the longer I could prevent him being removed and gone forever. As if part of him still lived on.

"What do you want to know? To be perfectly honest I don't feel there's anything I can add that will help in the slightest. It appears I know less than anybody about the life of my own husband. What was he doing here?" I asked aloud, into the sticky Kolkata air. "What were you doing here?" I asked again, this time quietly to Tom's body, running a hand gently over his cheek. "Help me to understand," I pleaded, while I cradled his face in my hands, his skin waxy and cold. It felt like any moment he may just wake and speak but the darkened eye lids gave no response as my tears splashed on his face. His solemn expression remained, unmoving and unreadable. I rubbed the tears away with my hand, almost fooling myself to believe that his tears were also falling and mingling with mine.

Roy shuffled gently from one foot to the other then lit a cigarette. Usually I hated smoking, but at present it was a familiar smell, something I could process and make sense of, unlike the smell of incense and decay. Roy seemed to read my thoughts and held out a cigarette to me. Despite not having smoked in years I reached out and took it, noticing how much my hand was shaking as I did so. Placing it between my lips Roy sparked the lighter and as the flame touched paper I drew heavily on the tobacco filled tube. The smoke tickled my chest making me cough, but I sucked on it twice more before throwing it to the ground then wiping my eyes and nose with my grubby sleeve. He pulled the packet from his pocket and placed one in his mouth offering another to me. I held up a hand to decline, feeling lightheaded with the heat and the effects of the cigarette.

Roy's phone beeped loudly, the sound startling me a little after getting used to the quiet. He tutted and quickly answered it, speaking loudly in Hindi or whatever language he used. He only spoke a matter of short sentences, sounding clearly annoyed at the disturbance, his free hand gesturing wildly as he talked. Once finished he popped the phone back in his trouser pocket then once more dabbed the sweat from his face with his handkerchief while shaking his head.

"Mrs Parker, did your husband have any childrens?" he asked suddenly, appearing agitated.

"Children?" I mournfully shook my head, suddenly feeling overwhelmed at how alone I now was. We had built our lives together, Tom was all I had and now that was gone. He was gone.

A stab of anger and resentment rose up in me directed at his cold corpse. The only thing I had ever truly wanted from him was to make us fully a family, to bring a life into this world together. So many nights when he was away I had lain alone in the empty bed, hands on my stomach, wishing that he would grant me that one thing to make our happiness complete and now he was gone and it was too late for that spark of him to live on in his child. Our child. The times I had begged him for the chance to become a mother. That was the one thing I had always yearned for, my body craved it. "How could you leave me on my own like this?" I shouted at his corpse. I had nothing left in this world.

"Mrs Parker. Did your husband have *other* children? Maybe from other womens?" Roy asked cryptically.

"No, he didn't have any children, from me or from anyone else."

"Are you quite sure?" he asked, eyeing me carefully and waving his cigarette in my direction.

"Of course I'm sure," I said, my temper rising. The

question almost seemed ironic when I considered Tom's stubbornness on the subject. I glanced back at the body, my mind drifting.

The weeks after our first date flew by, everything somehow seeming to take on a new significance. I was reawakened to my love of photography, seeing the beauty in everything and wanting to capture it in case that magic was ever to escape. By preserving it in graphic form it somehow became possible to hold a moment of perfection long after the time had passed. The possibility was always there to dust it off and relive that splendour again and again, the light and colour never to fade. I would snap everything, my senses heightened, grey areas in my life now vibrant and alive. I drove Tom crazy with the number of photos I took of us as a couple. Subliminally for the same reasons, to hold that perfection in case its beauty ever faded or changed as inevitably it always does.

Everything during those weeks seemed somehow to be enchanted and we would spend whole days together just talking and laughing. However, enchantments always break and I was subconsciously holding my breath for the moment when reality would burst the tender bubble we had created.

I vividly remember the week before our first Christmas when we were walking along in the park, lights glittering and children running past screaming. We were tottering along on the icy surface, slipping backwards and forwards, giggling at Tom's comment about us looking like a pair of new-born deer. Suddenly Tom's legs slipped this way then that and he ended up landing on the grass pulling me over on top of him. It was frosty and hard but after a shocked second we burst out laughing, much to the amusement of an elderly couple trudging past.

"Are you OK?" he asked wheezily, trying to get his breath back.

"Yeah, though I think I banged my arm," I pouted.

"Really?" he said picking it up gently and moving it to his lips. "Well, I shall just have to kiss it better then."

"Think I banged my lips too," I said smiling as he leaned in and kissed me, his cold nose rubbing my cheek.

"Mmmm, think that's all better now, though you can carry on if you want!" He smiled back at me and we lay there for a moment on the cold ground, just content to be in each other's presence. After a second I began to pull out my camera.

"What are you doing?" he asked, suddenly agitated.

"I just want to capture the magic of this moment. It's so perfect. Untouched snow, us, together. Do you think things will always be this perfect? This beautiful?" I asked, subconsciously pushing his hair behind his ear as I propped myself up on my elbow to view him better.

"I don't think there is such a thing as perfection. The word perfect, it's overused. I mean, no matter how good something is there is always something more which would make it even better. We can't box everything and label it perfect. Things are always changing, for better or worse," he stated, biting his thumb nail.

"I don't think I'm quite with you."

"Well, take for example a beautiful painting or picture in which everything is symmetrical and in place," he held up his hands as if taking the picture he described. "Because it's trapped as it is with people talking about it being amazing, it remains the same forever, you never know the potential it had. However, if something more was added to it if it could be even better; lighter colours here, more shadow there, whatever. We can't call it perfect because there is always the possibility to make it even better," he said philosophically, continuing to gaze at his imaginary picture.

"Like, when a couple have kids? I guess then you're making something really good even better," I mused. Instantly I felt his body tense next to mine. "Sorry, I wasn't hinting, I was just giving an example," I said. "I know it's far too soon to even be thinking about anything like that, I didn't mean to freak you out or anything!"

"You didn't freak me out," he said, his body loosening.

I breathed a silent sigh of relief and placed a kiss on his

cheek.

"It's not going to be an issue. I'm never going to have children. I think even considering bringing a child into this world is an act of cruelty," he said bluntly.

"What? What does that mean?" I asked, studying his face for a sign that he was joking.

"Well, just take a look around. Look at all the crap which goes on. Terrorism, murder, trafficking. Bringing a child into all of that is pure selfishness. Dragging something so innocent into a world of pain in which you can't always protect it, it's all messed up. If anything happens to the child, then it's your fault for choosing to create them in the first place." He stared past me into the distance.

"So you're saying that just because the world isn't completely and utterly perfect you wouldn't even consider having kids?" I asked, my voice rising at his obstinacy.

"In a word, yeah."

"How can you be so stubborn? So closed to the possibility of bringing a wonderful new life to the world? If you ask me, that's an act of cruelty." I fumed, wanting to cry as the perfect picture of us and our family that I had begun building in my head the last few weeks was shattered.

"Rachel, with all due respect, you have no idea what you're talking about. Nothing ever remains in this beautiful, magical, perfect state which you seem to be seeking. Things always get messed up."

"Not always," I said, placing my hand on his leg.

"Always," he said coldly, turning his face away and removing my hand.

We walked home in silence. The cold wind stung our cheeks as we pulled our coats tight around us in our individual worlds. The ice had now become an annoyance, slowing our walk to a crawl as we wanted to hurry home hoping that would thaw the frost that had developed between us in those past few moments. I looked mostly at my feet, trying to know what to read into Tom's comments as he stared off, eyes fixed steadily on a point in the distance. After a few moments I could no longer stand the tension.

"What are you thinking about?" I asked, linking my arm with his, trying to sound as cheerful as possible despite the sadness that was growing in my heart.

"Nothing much," he grunted, digging both hands into his pockets.

"Tom, please, let me in," I said, squeezing his arm tightly.

"Into what?" he asked, his jaw clenched.

"You. What's going on in here?" I said, tapping him gently on the forehead. "I need you to speak to me. Who knows, I might be able to help."

"Help? he snorted, touching his forehead. "How? It's a mess in here, I'm lost in here, there's no way you or anyone else can do anything."

"Please, if you would just try..."

"Listen, if you really want to help you'll just drop it. I don't want to talk about it," he said, then hunched up his shoulders plodding off, leaving me standing alone in the cold snow.

# Chapter Four

*Choosing to join the gang of Saiful Das and getting the tattoo, that was the moment in which I knew I was irretrievably lost. I was standing on a cliff edge and willingly throwing myself off. It was as if I had smashed my moral compass, leaving no way back to the person I was before. I guess that's how lying to you became easier, with no fixed moral point to refer back to.*

*I should never have allowed you in as far as you came, getting close to you, aware I could never give you the things you needed; stability, love, children. Things I should have provided, but no matter how hard I tried, or how sharp the pain in my heart at my failings, I couldn't. However, despite all that was taken from me that day, I could not have simply walked away. I had to gain entry to the gang, the brotherhood for one simple reason: To find my daughter.*

*Aisha was her name, meaning loved, protected. It now seems so ironic. She would be, will be twelve in October. I still don't know if I can use present or past tense. Life has revolved around that one wish, will be instead of would be. Hoping that there is a future and that I'm not just chasing shadows of the past.*

*To understand all that has happened I must begin by explaining my life, and the person I was before I met you. At eighteen I was young and naïve and set off around the world under the classic guise of 'finding myself'. I felt claustrophobic at home, an only child feeling myself forced into the legal profession by my Father. There was always that pressure to succeed, whatever I did was never quite good enough. The last three generations had all followed that route and there were pre-arranged contacts he had already made for me, 'You're a Parker my boy and the Law flows in your veins', that's what he always used to tell me. A respected profession, high earning and a welcome straight into the Old Boys club of my Father. What more could I want? I had the world at my feet. Success was just waiting for me to do the decent thing, head to the right Law school, shake hands with the right people and kiss the right arses.*

*But I wasn't ready for all that. 'Ungrateful' he called me, 'spiteful' 'a waster'. Who knows, maybe I was but I just needed room to breathe, to think about what it was I actually wanted from life. Three generations of Lawyers, all with as much money as they could want, fast cars, beautiful trophy wives and nice polite children but empty eyes and cold, bitter souls. I had never seen my Father totally care free, able to relax and spend time with Mum and me. He was always busy, always on the next case to bring in more money for a bigger house to fill with more new things we didn't need. To give him his due, he gave us all we needed financially, and he never hit me or my mother but there was no warmth, no care, no emotion, no love.*

*Maybe I was an idealist, destined to float around, but I wanted more than just an easy route to cash and a hernia operation in later life. I wanted to really live. To have a life full of passion, joy, love, new experiences. I wanted excitement, the unexpected, the unplanned. A life filled with amazing stories to tell other people. I guess that you should be careful what you wish for.*

*I'm not proud of it, but in the Summer before enrolling in University I took off, leaving only a note for my parents explaining that I was leaving to travel. I realise now that I was a coward and I simply ran away from that situation because I didn't want to deal with it. I tried standing up to him many times, saying I didn't know if that was what I wanted from life but it either ended in a shouting match about the disappointment I was to the family or worse still, the tense silence at each meal time, mum trying to make awkward conversation to hold us together. Even as I left the note I could hear his words of anger and disappointment ringing in my ears, his tone of voice clearly indicating he knew I would fail, that I was never good enough, driving me onwards to whatever destination I chose. My own free choices, able to go where I wished, see what I wanted, become the man I wanted to be and not moulded into the image of my Father. As I boarded the plane and the engine roared into action, for the first time in my life I felt released. Like a caged bird flying to whatever destiny I chose.*

*Since then though I feel as if I have always been running from something, never able to settle or stick to one thing: until Aisha arrived.*

*I had been on the move for a few months before I arrived in India. After a while in Thailand I had flown directly to Kolkata airport with nothing but a back pack full of dirty clothes, my passport and some traveller's cheques. I still remember the swell of excitement in my chest as I first touched down on the ground, the hazy heat almost too much for me. I felt an itch for adventure, a real sense that anything would be possible here with no commitments to hold me and nothing I had to move on to. As I rode into the city via taxi I noticed a sign swaying in the breeze, proudly declaring 'Welcome to Kolkata, the City of Joy'. The paradox was not lost on me that a family of six or seven had made their bed below that sign, looking at me with wild eyes of despair as the taxi stopped in traffic opposite them.*

*Within a few months I had discovered Kolkata for its endless beauty and its blazing grotesque, its amazement and horror, its shimmering hope and tragic despair. It felt like it had worked its way under my skin, becoming part of me; impossible to ever remove.*

*I easily managed to get a job teaching English in a Secondary School. The money was good, not too many responsibilities and well-disciplined children. I began to make some friends, but in a city of fourteen million where you are stared at like an attraction in the zoo on a daily basis I gradually began to feel an overwhelming loneliness. I felt isolated and as if I had cut all my ties from everything and everyone I knew. At nights I would dream of drifting aimlessly like a balloon, struck by the thought that if I were to die tomorrow there would be no-one at all to grieve my departure from this world.*

*It was in this self-pitying wallow that Layla came into my life. Through working at the school I had got to know a few people. She was a teacher, raised in a village just outside the main city. She was kind, funny and seemed to understand me like no-one else did despite the fact we were poles apart in our upbringing. Despite knowing the problems of social appearance, we began seeing each in secret. However, I was young, free and selfish, not really thinking about how much more she stood to lose than I did. I was always pushing her to take more risks, to forget about the social etiquette and prejudice, and to live life for the here and now, caring far more about myself than her. She, in return, was so smitten with me she would do whatever I asked.*

*After about five months of the relationship she wasn't at*

*work for a couple of days. Against her advice never to go to her apartment I went round to find her in her bed clothes with bloodshot eyes. She told me that she had found out she was pregnant. To be completely honest with you, my first reaction was pure selfishness in thinking what does this mean for me, followed by the quick deduction that it was simple enough for me to be on a plane away from here as soon as possible, leaving my new troubles behind me again as I headed for another nameless place. Sadly, it takes great effort for me not to still think like that. Even now, as your husband, my thought process often goes first to my self-preservation rather than being the man I wish I could be for you.*

*I stayed with her though, offering words of reassurance for hours and then headed home to check the next flight on to somewhere new, exotic and trouble free. However, as I scanned the airlines a voice inside me kept saying, 'when will you stop running little boy?' It was my moment to stop and be a man or to take another step on the road to being the kind of man I detested. For better or worse I decided I would stand by Layla and for the first time in my life try and put someone else before myself. I'm not going to say there weren't times before the birth when I didn't get itchy feet and wish to be as far away as possible from the situation, but over those few months, seeing Layla in all her vulnerability I grew to love her completely, hating myself for my earlier thoughts.*

*It was an extremely difficult time, especially for Layla coping with being unmarried and pregnant from a foreigner, or gora as I was often called. During the whole time she did not tell anyone from back home in the village fearing that she may be disowned or worse. Still I tried to persuade her that they were family and would accept her no matter what, but I was still being a naïve little boy assuming that positive thinking would make it all better; it didn't.*

*A few months after the birth things had settled down and we were able to begin our lives together as a family in my small apartment. We were a unit, but still it constantly felt like we could not fully enjoy everything without Layla receiving the acknowledgement she craved from her family. Having shunned my parents and severed ties I didn't want her to make the same mistake so I managed to talk Layla into going back to the village to speak to her family. It was clear how important it was to her to have their approval and it felt like once she had that we could move on and begin to become a proper family.*

*After it was decided she booked the travel for the next evening. I saw the fear in her eyes before she left and wanted to be there to comfort her, but knew the shame that would already be raised by having a child, let alone a child from a gora.*

*She set off leaving me terrified about coping with a two*

*month old baby in the middle of a strange city, vowing to be back in a week after she had the chance to sort things out and seek a blessing from her parents. I put her on a coach to the village that night.*

*It was the last time Aisha or I ever saw her mother.*

## Chapter Five

"So, Mrs Parker, you are telling me for the honest truth that you and your husband had no childrens and that he did not have any with any other womens? This is very interesting," Superintendent Roy said, sucking once more on his cigarette and running his fingers over his greasy moustache. A mosquito landed on his neck and he effortlessly trapped it between his thumb and forefinger. He ground his fingers together and then inspected them with intrigue before wiping them on his trousers.

"Of course it's the honest truth, why exactly would I lie about something like that?" I said, anger and frustration rising in me. I placed my fingers to my throbbing temples. I just wanted to be alone to begin my grieving but instead I had to face these ridiculous questions which seemed intended to apply pressure to the most sensitive parts of me.

"I have not said that *you* were lying Mrs Parker. Not yet. Is there any chance that your husband was not telling you something?" he asked, arching his eyebrows.

"I'm pretty sure that during the three years we were married that would have been something which may have come up in conversation, don't you?" I said, my voice dripping with exhausted sarcasm.

"Just like he mentioned this trip to India to you? I am sure your husband was very honest man with nothing to be hiding Mrs Parker," Roy said, a self-satisfied grin touching the right hand side of his face. "If you will be forgiving me I may not believe everything which you tell me about your husband. I will take it, as you English say, with a pinch of the salt." With that he tossed the cigarette on to the ground, took a pencil from his shirt pocket and made a few notes in a small black book, the pages of which were yellowed with use and curled at the corners. Once finished he placed the pencil in his mouth and began to chew on the end of it.

I wanted to open my mouth to bite back at Roy in Tom's defence but no words came. I hated to admit it but Roy was right. Anything I could tell him about Tom, anything I had known as fact had now entered an ambiguous grey area Nothing from our life together could explain to me why he would be here. Nothing made any sense. I was no longer certain of anything about him, about us, at all. I couldn't have even sworn that Tom Parker was his real name.

My eyes scanned Tom's face trying to dredge up old memories like a trawler in the ocean searching for treasure. I needed certainty and searched for a memory from our life to provide a base on which to hang my reality of our time together.

My mind raced back to when we had been together for about three months. During that time we had been on many dates and I had cooked for him numerous times but despite my constant hinting I had never received an invitation to his apartment. I decided that I needed to be more assertive and one evening headed to his house. I rang the bell and a few moments later a very surprised Tom peeled back a curtain and stared out, like a nervous child waiting to go on stage at a pantomime. I smiled and waved at him, then without returning either affection he disappeared behind the curtain. After an awkward few moments with me standing on his porch unsure if he was coming, the door creaked open and Tom's head shot out, his neck winding from around the frame like a tortoise afraid to leave his shell. He blinked a few times, lost for words.

"Hey honey," I said stepping up and placing a kiss on his cheek. "Thought I would pop round and surprise you. I've been curious to see what it looks like round here and I was beginning to think I would be waiting till next year before I got an invite, so, here I am!" He scratched his neck then rubbed his earlobe, a trait I had noticed he did whenever he felt uncomfortable. He made no move to welcome me in, an awkward silence settling between us.

"Well, do we have to stand out here all night? Can I come in?" I asked, maintaining as cheerful a voice as possible.

"Now is probably not the best time," he said hurriedly, "I was just, doing some, you know..." he said, his voice trailing off.

My suspicion was aroused, wondering what he could be trying to hide. I stepped up to the door to force myself inside, but he continued to stand, blocking the way. "Tom, what's up? Why won't you let me in? Have I done something wrong?"

He shook his head apologetically. "No, you have done nothing wrong at all." He looked at his feet, refusing to meet my eye.

"Well what is it?" In my mind only one option appeared to be left. "Is there someone else here with you? Have you been seeing someone else?" I asked, bracing myself for his answer.

"No! Rachel, no! I can't believe you would think that. It's just, well, it's not much to look at, you know?" he sighed as he stepped aside to let me past. I barged in, eagerly glancing around to try and find the source of his discomfort. But there was nothing. Literally, nothing. All that the ground floor flat consisted of was a bedroom which had a white sheet on the bed and a few clothes scattered around, a living room which had one chair, an empty pot noodle and a kitchen which had a frying pan and one small saucepan. There was no sign of decoration, no posters, pictures, books. Nothing which would distinguish it from anywhere else. I had seen travelodges with more character.

"I like what you've done with the place," I said, laughing nervously. He wandered around collecting up the pot noodle, muttering about not having got round to decorate, although I knew that he had been here for at least a year.

It was an eerie sensation not seeing a single photo of family, friends or celebrations. No connection with the past or any other human being. As a photographer my whole life was about capturing memories and here was a world Tom had created, devoid of history. It felt tragic seeing a home so lifeless and bare. I awkwardly perched on the arm of the chair and looked around, trying to find something positive to comment on but failed. He stood, hands in his pockets as he rocked back and forth on his heels, looking at the ground. In honesty, he had never spoken about his parents and did not mention friends from his past but I assumed there would be some kind of clue here to help me swim deeper into my understanding of him.

"So," I said, trying to think of something to break the uncomfortable silence. "You like the minimalistic look."

"Makes cleaning easy," he joked, then his brow creased. "Listen, Rachel. There's something I need to tell you. Before you... I..." he paused, looking around the room, his eyes settling on something directly in front of him. There was a heaviness in his voice that felt like he was having to heave the words up from a hidden place. "Well, my life was totally different. I messed a lot of things up and I was messed up by a lot of things," he paused, considering what depth to go into, then just shrugged and threw his arms up in an expression of defeat. "I'm not proud of who I was. Not much from my past makes me smile, so I don't like reminders of it." His face shifted, as if a dark cloud had passed over and left a clear, bright sky. "But you came along and made it all good." I knelt before him and he took my face in his strong hands, pressing his forehead against mine. "I need you babe. Promise you won't ever leave me?"

"I promise," I whispered, gently running my hand through his hair.

He breathed deeply then pulled back, forcing a smile to his face. "Right, how about something to eat? I make a mean pot noodle?"

I smiled back, pleased at being given a snap shot into his past, a little more of the background in the picture of his mysterious life.

At the time I didn't realise that was one of the only occasions on which I would voluntarily hear of his existence before 'us' and wished that I had pushed for more detail, more stories. I constantly told myself that one day he would be ready to open up, like an orchid coming from the darkness to flower and reveal all, but that time never came and now I know, it never will.

I tried to allow myself to be distracted by the thought of food, but as I stood I traced where his eyes had rested and noticed something to which I had been oblivious before. In the middle of this empty, white room sat a green, child's shoe isolated on a shelf. I looked at Tom questioningly, wondering why he kept something so bizarre when all else had been discarded. He shrugged his shoulders and again rubbed his earlobe.

"I've had it for many years. I guess you could call it, ah, my good luck charm. It reminds me to be a better man and I need reminding of that often," he said, turning and heading towards the kitchen. In all the times I visited after that, the shoe was never again on display, though I knew Tom kept it stored away in his bedside table for all the years we were married. I wondered momentarily if his lucky charm had been with him the night he was killed and if so what had become of it as he now lay here with no more to hide behind than a bloodied bed sheet.

I stood looking at Tom's naked body, wondering for a moment what they had done with his clothes and possessions. Would they be able to shed some light on his reason for being here? Some sort of clue to help me understand? As the thoughts continued to mist across my mind I became aware of Roy continued watching me with his beady eyes, expectant of answers.

"You see Mrs Parker, you are asking yourself the same questions. How is it that you are to be trusting words which you have been told when most of it is probably being lies. What I am needing is facts from you. I need to be making as much information as possible to be finding out what has happened here. What can you be telling me about his family?" he asked, once more dabbing his brow with his handkerchief.

I shook my head, unable to comment as I had never met them, Tom keeping that part of his life very private. Roy raised an inquisitive eyebrow.

"This shaking means that they are dead? All of them? How can this be?"

"No, not dead. I just never met them," I said, looking shamefully at my hands. "Tom fell out with his parents years ago so we were never introduced," I said, mournful that I was denied the possibility of becoming part of his family. I would have loved the chance to go to family celebrations, to have them involved in our lives, but Tom was too stubborn, refusing point blank to even speak of them.

"What is this, fell out?" Roy asked, wrinkling his eyebrows in confusion.

"It means they didn't get along. They argued a lot and were no longer speaking to each other." Roy's eyebrows now arched wide in disbelief as he shook his head.

"But this is how it is in the family. People argue and fight but it does not mean they are not speaking to each other. There must have been some most bad fighting for this to happen?" he probed. I shrugged my shoulders, hazy on the details of why there had been such a separation over so long a time.

"This I cannot understand. What kind of man is this who can disown his family? The people who gave him life and brought him into this world."

"It's sad but Tom thought it was for the best. I couldn't change his mind." I said, shrugging again.

"This is a most terrible thing. Without family a man is nothing. Marriage is the uniting of both families, not just the couple. This cannot be happening this way." He sucked his teeth then looked at me. "If you are not even meeting his family then I am sure there are most dark things about your husband which you are not knowing."

# Chapter Six

*Days turned into weeks and weeks into months. Every moment that passed the hope of Layla returning grew dimmer and dimmer. After two months I struggled to even remember what she had looked like.*

*In those first months after her leaving I am honestly not sure if I ever slept. Every night Aisha would wake and scream for comfort. I would always be awake already though, the urgency of her screams were about the only thing which would focus my mind and stop my thoughts spiralling down a well of despair, knowing that I somehow had to hold it all together for her.*

*I was constantly on edge, fearful of what was happening with Layla and why I had not heard anything from her. Every time the phone rang or there was a knock at the door my heart raced, but it was never her. I felt so useless, separated from her with no way of knowing how she was or what she was thinking or feeling. That combined with trying to raise our child in an unfamiliar country without a clue what I was doing almost drove me insane. Every day I worried about how I was looking after her. Was she sleeping enough? Was she sleeping too much? Was she too hot? Too cold? Did she have enough milk? Was I winding her properly? I needed her mother there to guide me, show me how to do it all properly. I was terrified of doing something wrong to this precious new life and felt so ill equipped to provide even her basic needs.*

*My feelings later turned to desperation as I wondered if Layla had just decided to leave Aisha and me to start a new life back in the village or in another city. Had the love between us not been true? Had I made it more than it was in my mind? Had she found someone else? Been married off by her family? I feared she had chosen not to return and began to feel more and more like she had chosen her freedom above us, resentment taking root in my heart.*

*Finally the desperation turned to despondency as every moment was spent considering and reconsidering why she had not returned. I had read stories back at home of girls killed by their family for bringing shame, so called 'honour killings' and feared the worst. I prayed these stories were an exaggeration and a rarity and that she was still on her way back to us, but by the time Aisha was eight months old any hope had gone and whether it was her choice or not I knew that it was Aisha and me left alone, to try and make it by ourselves. I had no idea of the name of the village Layla had gone to, making it impossible to try and find her, especially with having a small child to take on the journey. It felt like giving up but I did not know what else I could do.*

*As you can imagine, life was not easy. Looking back on it, I can't remember how exactly we survived those first few months, but somehow we struggled through. In those early dark days I viewed Aisha as a restrictive burden, like a cage around me taking my freedom or an anchor around my neck, preventing me from moving. I feel so ashamed now that I had those feelings towards her, but this is the time for me to tell you the whole truth even if I would rather not remember it.*

*In her dependency though she soon became my whole world. Rather than a weight restricting my movements she had become an anchor which held me firm through the storms I endured. She had given meaning to my life and rather than just floating like an empty vessel I now had purpose, a reason for existing. Someone to stop me caring about only myself and completely changing my perspective on life. Every day I grew to love her more, rejoicing in the small developments she made, but wishing Layla was there to share in them too.*

*She was an unbelievably beautiful child with thick black hair, smooth light brown skin and the most striking emerald green eyes I have ever seen. I would just sit and watch her playing for hours feeling such a sense of love, wanting to give her the very best in life as I guess all parents do. I think that raising her by myself created such a strong sense of duty and responsibility, that all we had in this world was each other. We were a little island cast away from the rest of the world, having to survive by ourselves.*

*I still had friends from the teaching job, but as I was*

*unable to continue working or socialising my circle of friends shrank dramatically. Most were in India for a maximum of six months and didn't really count baby sitting as the most exciting thing to do in such an amazing country. Some came to visit at the start, bringing meals and helping out but even the most dedicated began to dwindle as my company became so difficult, sleep deprivation and fear over the disappearance of Layla not making for great conversation. I didn't blame them and knew that I would have been exactly the same in their position. I guess in some ways I was in such a state it was almost a relief not to have to make any effort to socialise. It meant I didn't have to say out loud what I was dealing with. All of my time was consumed reading baby books, heating up milk and changing nappies within a small apartment. We were so consumed in each other it felt there was no longer space for anyone else in our lives.*

*As you may have guessed, money soon began to run low and I had no real way of bringing it in; free time was not something that existed for me anymore and child benefits were unheard of. After a few months I made the difficult decision of swallowing my pride and contacting my mum. I had hit the bottom and had no way of providing for Aisha without her help. It was the first time since I had left that I had spoken to her, shame having stopped me making contact.*

*Despite trying to persuade me that I should, she agreed*

*not to tell my Father and regardless of the circumstances she was excited about having this new granddaughter. I managed to receive regular cash from her without my Father noticing as the 'Parker pockets go deep'. Despite her almost begging me to return so that they could help look after Aisha I remained too proud and declined a return flight for us both which she pleadingly offered. I still could not face heading home and feeling my Father's stinging criticism and complete lack of understanding. I could already see the look on his face and wanted to be spared from that humiliation, telling myself that we could make it on our own and that it was better for her to be raised here; a decision that still haunts me.*

*When Aisha reached eight months I knew something had to change. After all the desperation and waiting for Layla to come back I finally admitted to myself that she was gone for good and that I could not continue to sit in the small apartment amidst Aisha's screams, fantasizing she would return. I took some of the money which mum had sent over and we moved to a bigger apartment across the city, the move symbolising a new beginning for Aisha and me, a life no longer defined by waiting but on moving forward. I decided it was time to sort myself out so that I could be a better father, recognising it was time to start looking after myself properly if I was to look after Aisha. I hired an Ayah, or female maid to help with cooking and cleaning, jobs that I had seriously neglected over the last six months, my ribs beginning to protrude beneath my cotton shirts. Within a week I had no idea how I had coped before and actually managed to find time to relax and sleep, a luxury which I had long gone without.*

*It took a few weeks for me to actually allow the Ayah, called Shakti, to help with looking after Aisha as I had grown so over protective of her. Every time she cried during the day and Shakti moved to help her I would leap up and rebuke her, not allowing her to carry out the main duty of most Ayahs. Slowly though I learned to give over responsibility to Shakti and I grew to cherish the freedom to be able to go out for a walk or even visit some of the sights of the city. I felt like a bear waking from hibernation. I was able to raise my head from my slumber and realise that life was about more than just dogged survival.*

*I felt like I had aged fifty years over the last few months but that my childish joy was slowly coming back. Seeing Aisha giggle and begin to crawl filled me with such delight that I just wanted to sing and dance. It felt like we had made it, life was manageable and I was no longer living in fear. Shakti had raised the children of three different Swaamis and had a wealth of knowledge of different coughs and cries of different babies, which put my mind as much at ease as it could be about her development.*

*During this time I managed to get a part time job teaching English to some rich kids in another part of town, bringing in enough money to cover our rent and food and even enough to begin with paying a token amount back to mum each month. I got more used to the customs in Kolkata, growing to love the haggling and the local food and chai. I enrolled in Hindi lessons so that I would be able to teach Aisha although by the age of three she was far more fluent than me from growing up with Shakti always present. She was incredibly bright and just seemed to take everything in her stride. Her caramel skin and piercing green eyes made her a real attraction every time we left the house and we would be mobbed by admirers making simple tasks like shopping often an exhausting affair. By the age of five she was brimming with confidence, but had none of the arrogance that I had found in many of the children which I taught.*

*For the first time in my life I felt almost content. Nearly complete. As if all the pieces in the puzzle were coming together, although there was always a mother shaped hole which Aisha now seemed to be realising. The question of 'why haven't I got a mummy like the other children?' became more difficult to answer as her understanding of life became greater, leaving me to mumble things about heaven and mummy not having been well as the easiest way to explain things beyond my understanding. My mind was still plagued with how I could have done things differently. If only I hadn't sent her back to her family. Should I have tried to find her? Should I have alerted the Police? For the most part though I managed to justify my actions, silencing the voices to find contentment in my life with Aisha.*

*The future had now become something solid, something to look forward to rather than simply enduring each day. This was highlighted in some of my conversations with Aisha. From very young she had many ideas of her hopes and dreams, beginning as a Dinosaur, to a Unicorn and then a Princess, all dreams of a bright future. A few days after her fifth birthday we were sitting below a makeshift tent in the living room comprising of bed sheets and cushions eating a snack Shakti had prepared for us.*

*"Daddy, I don't want to be a Princess anymore when I grow up," she suddenly declared. "They just have lots of money and sit in their castles all day. Mummy's gone to heaven and maybe if I had been a Doctor or someone who helps people I could have saved her, so I want to be a Doctor so that I can help people and make things all better when they get bad. Then people won't be sad when the people they love go away," she said as she continued to draw a picture of what she thought her mummy would have looked like.*

*I leaned over and kissed her on the top of the head, tears streaming down my face. "You can be whatever it is you want to be my little Princess," I said, swearing in my heart to make whatever sacrifices it would take so that she could achieve her dreams. "Follow your dreams and they will come true, I'll make sure of it," I vowed.*

*Sadly though, despite our best intentions and what we thought was our best effort our dreams are sometimes stolen from us.*

*It was three days after that conversation that we had headed down to one of the bustling markets to pick up a new salwar kameez for Aisha as she was beginning to outgrow most of her clothes.*

*Every single moment of the day is now etched in my mind in high definition. It was during monsoon season and we had chosen a time when all clouds had disappeared and the sun was blazing down. Aisha was wearing an emerald green salwar kameez which was decorated with shining silver sequins and matching green shoes. She wore a plastic necklace with pink jewels on it and on her wrist she proudly sported a green and pink rakhi, or bracelet, which I had made for her a few days ago and she had not taken off since. I had seen some of the Hindus we worked with where the sisters would give their brothers a rakhi as a symbol for protection in the year to come, so as her only family I made her one when she asked about them.*

*The market stalls were vibrant as always, with fruit sellers hollering as we walked past, trying to beckon us over. We regularly went to the market and were reasonably well recognised by some of the wallahs (or sellers) on the market. One or two would now stop and chat, mostly asking after Aisha and her health, often offering her small presents from their stall which she would take gratefully and thank them repeatedly while standing behind my legs.*

*We had just entered into the main section of the market and I was gripping Aisha's hand tightly due to the sheer volume of people, many staring at us, others offering their services in carrying our goods or else asking for a few rupees. We had become skilled in the art of keeping our heads down in these scenarios and made it into the covered section of the market, Aisha running to keep pace next to me. We stopped by a fruit stall, a wallah eagerly offering his services. The smell of the fresh fruit in the heat of the day was intoxicating.*

*I leafed through my wallet and found two silver rupee coins, dropping them into the wrinkled hands of the ancient wallah. He thanked me and placed a giant slice of watermelon into each of my hands. I looked down and Aisha was smiling broadly at me. Watermelon was her current favourite which she would eat for every meal if possible. I was about to pass it down to her when I heard a crack of thunder from above us. I looked along the row of market stalls and saw the monsoon rain lashing down, steam rising as it hit the hot ground. Wallahs outside began to scramble around, throwing sheets of tarpaulin over their wares for protection. A sudden swell of customers squeezed their way into the covered area, two particularly large women in sari's jostling between Aisha and me.*

*I looked around to see her being swept up by the human tide that was surging past us. She reached out her hands to me, eyes wide with panic as a group of young boys ran into the space between us, playfully punching each other on the arms. I instantly dropped the watermelon and began to push my way through the crowd, my eyes fixed on her green top as it bobbed up and down and legs cut across obscuring my vision. I called her name and began shouting in a desperate panic.*

*As I pushed through the crowd it suddenly seemed to part and I saw Aisha looking around wildly about five foot in front of me. I called her name and she looked up.*

*"Daddy!" she screamed, arms reached out as the tears rolled down her cheeks. My heart started to beat again as I began to bend over to pick her up when suddenly I felt two rough hands shove me in the side, causing me to topple straight over into a stall packed with fruit. I landed awkwardly on my elbow, oranges and mangoes rolling into the alleyway, causing shouts from an angry wallah and*

*laughter from the young boys. I looked around, but whoever had done it disappeared undetected like smoke into the large crowd.*

*I looked up to see a man in his early thirties grabbing Aisha around the waist and pulling her backwards through the crowd. She screamed and kicked out, flailing around her little limbs to be released but it was to no avail due to his superior strength. The man had on dark shades, hair gelled down from a centre parting and was in a bright white vest, revealing a muscular torso. Two other men were next to him, both in white cotton t-shirts and jeans. He spun around and all I could see were Aisha's legs frantically flying around as he dashed through the crowd, a tattoo proudly displaying an eagle with a snake in its claw on his left shoulder blade.*

*Immediately I leapt to my feet and pursued them, knocking people over as I pushed to gain ground. However, they obviously knew the market well and managed to move quickly, despite carrying Aisha. They flew around the first corner, scattering two giant wicker baskets of fish and ice over the ground to slow my progress. As I negotiated my way through the mess I could see them ahead, knocking angry market goers out of the way as they ran. They disappeared into a clothes stall and I chased through, hoping they had trapped themselves. However, as I entered I saw the back of one of the men disappearing through a curtain at the rear. I continued chasing, my heart bursting in my chest as I followed through the curtain and into the street, the rain still lashing down.*

*Due to the rain the usually bustling streets were near empty and it was easy to spot the three men turning the next corner. One of them slipped, landing in the road before being hauled to his feet by the other in the white t-shirt. However, he looked injured and was limping as he tried to keep running. Like a beast in the wild I smelled weakness and pushed on, knowing if I could at least catch him I would have a way to get Aisha. As they turned the next corner I was gaining on them, the blood vessels sounding like they would burst in my ears as I charged on through the pouring rain, the water stinging my eyes. They turned another corner and I was within thirty feet of them, nearing at every second. They nipped through a small, deserted alleyway. As I entered the short passage I could see them emerging from the other side of it. They seemed to be slowing and I felt my hopes soar. They had given up. They knew I would catch them.*

*As quickly as my hopes had risen they plummeted as I realised there was a car at the end of the alleyway waiting for their arrival. The back door flew open and the men jumped straight in to the car, the third hobbling and managing to slam the door just as I arrived at the car. I grabbed for the handle and pulled as if my life depended on it but it was locked. Through the window I could see the three men crammed into the back of the taxi, with Aisha in the middle of them, still shaking to get free. I reached out my hand to bang on the window when the car began to speed off.*

*As it pulled away I gave chase, banging my fist against the rear of the car as it gathered pace. I managed to stay with it as it slowed to turn a corner, Aisha's face turned to look at me, her pleading eyes locked on mine asking to save her before a hand grabbed her head and pulled her down. I tried to grab hold of the rear of the car but my hands slipped straight off in the rain. As I stumbled it accelerated, pulling away from me. I continued to blindly chase but soon all that I could see were the blinking rear lights reflecting on the road in the distance before they too vanished from sight.*

*Exhausted, I tripped and fell, landing on my knees on the pavement, splattered and soaked as I just stared helplessly into the distance where the car had gone.*

*The newly made monsoon river continued to rush by me. Suddenly, something in the water caught my eye. A delicate green shoe was being swept along amongst the other debris. It was Aisha's shoe. I picked it up and pulled it tightly into my chest, cradling it as I had cradled Aisha as a baby. I put my head in my hands trying to understand all that had just happened, the crushing desperation almost overwhelming me.*

*As the rain lashed down I felt soulless, as if every particle of me could just come apart and be washed away in to the drainage system. I sat motionless as the rain drops pounded me like bullets. What was the point in living now? How could I go on? I brought her small shoe to my lips and gently kissed it.*

*A new resolve came to me. I had lost her mother and had gone down without a whimper. Not this time. I would fight. I would do whatever it took to find my precious baby girl and once I did I would make them pay for this. I vowed that they would suffer for taking her.*

## Chapter Seven

My tired mind was swirling with doubts and confusion. It felt like a dense fog had covered everything I once knew to be true and I was straining to distinguish reality from imagination. I needed time to think, time to sort out my head and escape this insanity. There was just too much to process, I felt like I was about to break down.

I began walking towards the rusted door of the basement, heading for the bright daylight that lay above.

"Mrs Parker, to where are you going?" Roy asked, strategically placing the pencil behind his ear as his hand dropped to his side.

"I just need some air, it's so stifling down here. I need to sort my head out," I said, about to walk out when I noticed his hand resting on the revolver in his belt.

"I am afraid that leaving is not an option in this very moment," he said, making sure I saw his gesture by strumming his fingers on the butt of his gun. His eyes were alert and clear daring me to continue.

I defensively threw my hands in the air, "are you going to shoot me?" I asked now totally exhausted and baffled.

"No, no Mrs Parker. I just need to be assuring your full co-operation. I am here with a job to do as you will understand. Now please, if you will come back in we can continue to talk nicely on these things," he said, offering what he appeared to think was a placating smile but which gave him a slightly manic look, especially after threatening to pull a gun on me seconds before.

"OK, OK," I said hoarsely, my arms still in the air as I walked slowly back in to the room to be sure not to give him any excuse to use his revolver. "You're the boss. I just wanted some air. I am sure you can appreciate it's been a rough day," I said, glancing from Roy's gleaming revolver to the bullet wounds on Tom's body on the table only a few feet away. "I thought I was just here to identify the body. I assumed that I was free to leave at any stage as I was helping with enquiries. That's how it works isn't it?" I said, my voice full of frustration as I felt close to fainting, the stifling heat seeming to have intensified as I watched Roy, completely unsure of his next move.

"Yes, yes. It is just helping with these enquiries," he said dismissively, removing his hand from the revolver and pointing for me to sit on the rickety wooden chair in the corner of the room. "Maybe a seat will help as good as some air, yes? As long as you are helping then there is no need to be scared. No-one will be getting hurt." He held up his hands as a sign of peace, then gestured again for me to be seated.

"But you're saying I can't leave?" I asked, as I wiped the dusty seat and tentatively sat down, worried that I would collapse if I didn't sit soon.

"You are free to leave at any time Mrs Parker but it would be best for you to be staying and answer the questions. As you are imagining there are many of these questions about your husband and it may look very suspicious if you are not willing to be helping the police. We are here to help you. We are wanting to catch whoever has killed your husband but need your help to be doing that. Without your help there may be problems coming your way Mrs Parker. Are you understanding me?" he said, stroking the top of his revolver for emphasis on the final sentence, his bulging eyes locked with mine. I swallowed hard, feeling like an animal coaxed into a cage suddenly hearing the metal door clanging shut behind it.

"I assume there's no chance of me getting a lawyer?" I asked through dry lips.

Roy threw back his head and chuckled a wheezy, rasping laugh which evolved into a minor coughing fit. He wiped his mouth with the sleeve of his tattered brown uniform then squatted next to me looking directly into my eyes, so close that I could see the beating pulse in the side of his head. "But Mrs Parker, if you are telling the truth surely there is no need for this lawyer? You are helping me and I am helping you. We do not need anybody else to be getting in the way of that. Now, let's stop this games and start getting to the understanding of what has happened."

"Ok, but I have already told you, I don't know anything about what has happened." I said wearily, resting my head in my hands.

"Mrs Parker, there is an easy way to be doing this and also a very hard one too," Roy said walking towards me as he unclipped his handcuffs and let them swing menacingly at his waist.

"Honestly, I want to help! I just don't know anything!" I said, almost screaming, panic starting to rise at the thought of being trapped. I leapt to my feet but he was already standing over me.

"Tut tut," he said, sucking air through his crooked teeth. "It is a shame it must be the hard way," he said, roughly grabbing my forearms as I fought against him, but he had done this a million times before and it was no use. He forcefully closed the solid handcuff over my wrists, almost tight enough to cut off the circulation before straightening up and placing the key in his shirt pocket.

The handcuffs reached through the back of the chair, securing me to it, my arms pulled behind me. The hot metal nipped my skin as I screamed back, "I told you I don't know anything you crazy son of a bitch!" while banging my feet like a child in a tantrum as I tried to wrench myself free. Screaming, I shook the chair, violently rattling the handcuffs.

Roy grabbed my face tightly between his nicotine stained

fingers and pulled it up towards him, his long yellowed nails digging in to my cheeks. His foul breath was warm on my face as he breathed heavily on me.

"That is no way to speak to a Police Officer," he said smugly, a cruel smile again playing on his face. "Now, you will tell me all you know or things will be getting more difficult," he said, spitting the words out from between his gritted teeth. He pushed my head back making my neck snap, then straightened himself, folding his arms. After staring at me for a moment he unfolded his arms and removed his final cigarette, screwed up the packet and tossed it at my feet. Already I could feel a bruise rising on my wrists from the tightness of the handcuffs, but this did not stop me trying again to twist free of them but it seemed the harder I wriggled the tighter they became. It was warm and wet around the cuffs and I was unsure if it was pure sweat or whether I had struggled so much the handcuffs had cut into my skin and I was bleeding.

Despite everything rational in me saying to keep still, I attempted to free myself once more with all my might. The chair was not as sturdy as the handcuffs though and there was a loud crack as one of the legs gave way causing me to topple sideways, landing on my left shoulder on the unforgiving floor. An immense pain shot through my left arm and bright lights flashed in my head as I shrieked. For a moment I lost consciousness.

My grazed face stung as I slowly woke on the uneven concrete. For a moment the pain in my shoulder was dull and distant then came back in all its might. Groggily I looked around, becoming aware of my surroundings as a cockroach scurried over my right arm, the tickle of its legs making me shudder. As I lay cuffed to the broken wooden chair my tears began to flow. My shoulders shook as far as the handcuffs would allow while I sobbed, sending bolts of pain from my shoulder through me each time I moved.

The tears were not from the pain though. They were from a woman who had reached the point of exhaustion, had lost her husband and was now being arrested for something about which she knew absolutely nothing, in a place with no one at all to help her. It felt like the whole rug that I had built my life on had been whipped out from under me, exposing the decayed foundations I had been a fool to build on.

Eventually I managed to gain control over the sobs, having to fight back the tears to prevent the pain in my arm from overwhelming me.

"Have you quite finished Mrs Parker?" a voice above me sneered. Cigarette ash floated on to the floor around me like the residue of an explosion. I had to twist my neck up to see Roy standing to the right of me. From my mangled position on the floor I could take in his scuffed shoes, starched brown trousers and revolver. The trouser leg stopped a good inch before his shoes, exposing his bony ankle.

"Please, just let me go. I have already told you, I know nothing," I said in a whisper, directed more at the floor than at Roy. I dropped my head back to the ground.

"You see Mrs Parker, I am wanting to be believing you, most definitely. More than most in the world I am wanting to let you go. But I'm afraid that things are not this simple. As you have been telling me, he was your husband and after three years marriage you should be knowing many things about him and it is most important we know these things and are able to find anyone else who knows about your husband and his work."

"His work? What do you mean? All I know is that Tom was a salesman in an insurance firm. Seems like you know far more than me." I tried to look up at Roy to read his expression but could see no further than his waist. My eyes were swollen and sore and my nose was running, mingling with the sweat which stuck strands of hair across my face. I sniffed, but it was a futile attempt to stop it.

"Your husband was well known here in Kolkata, Mrs Parker. In fact, he had many people here looking for him. The Police in particular are very interested in your husband. Very interested indeed. Your husband was known to us for working in one of the very biggest gangs here and also for murder," he stated bluntly.

"Murder? You liar! He could never have been. In some sort of gang? How was he meant to do that between nipping out to work in the morning and coming home at night? My husband could never have killed anyone!" The rage that overtook me was for the slander of the gentle man who I loved, but even as I was screaming at Roy there was still a part of me that was so unnerved by all that had happened that I wasn't sure what to believe anymore. But murder? Never. Those loving hands that had held me. Surely they couldn't have been used to end someone's life. I shuddered and pushed the thought away. Not Tom. Not my Tom. No matter what lies I was fed here, there was no chance that I could believe that of him.

"Why are you telling me these lies?" I shouted, straining my neck to direct my anger at Roy. He crouched down and all I could see were his knobbly knees protruding through his worn trousers as I heard a small cough and then the sound of paper rustling.

"Lies? Lies you are thinking Mrs Parker? Perhaps I have something which will be changing your mind".

My stomach turned as I tried to figure out what he could possibly be looking for to prove his point. Before I could guess, three photos were dropped on the ground in front of me, the dust rising and stinging my eyes. I coughed and blinked rapidly.

"If you will be looking, I think something may be of interest to you here Mrs Parker," he said as he fanned the three photos out so that all were visible from my limited viewpoint on the dusty floor. I gasped in horror as the first picture came into focus. In it was an Indian man wearing only a pair of jeans lying face down on the ground, his hair sprawled out behind him. It was taken in what looked like a deserted side street amongst numerous cardboard boxes and plastic bags. About two foot in front of him was a gun lying in the middle of the road. His back had three bullet wounds almost in a straight line running down his spine, only inches apart. His torso was shadowed with a thick line of dark red blood. My mind raced. Was Tom supposed to have killed this man? This could be anybody. It proved nothing I reasoned to myself.

I looked at the second picture, again an Indian man, this time the picture only showing his torso, leaving it to the imagination what had happened to his severed head. The third was again another Indian, this time with bleached hair which had gone a strong shade of orange. Like the others he had a naked torso and there were several knife wounds through his back. I shuddered and looked away.

"Why have you shown me these? What are they meant to show about Tom? They prove nothing, regardless of whatever sick story you want to spin about them. They could be anybody," I stated, trying to block the gruesome images from my mind.

"Please, look again Mrs Parker. Perhaps you will notice something they have in common," Roy urged.

"They're all dead? Yeah I figured that one out on the first look thanks," I spat back at him.

"No, *look*," he said, pointing to the first photo. I glanced over and suddenly I realised what he was hinting at. I exhaled deeply and would have collapsed if I wasn't already on the floor. Then, reluctantly, I looked at the second and third for confirmation.

On the back of each of the three men was a tattoo of an eagle with a snake in its claws. Exact replicas of the one which Tom had. I looked up, wild eyed at Roy. He smiled back at my comprehension.

"Perhaps now you see I am not the one who is being the liar," he said, his smirk looking even more sinister from my horizontal position.

"But, what are they? Why? I mean, who..." I asked, the words tumbling over each other and out of my mouth.

"So this tattoo is familiar to you, yes? Well, it is also very familiar to the police here in Kolkata Mrs Parker. As I mentioned, this tattoo shows that these men are part of a gang, a brotherhood. They have made a pact to be becoming like family to each other. To look out for each other, protect each other, kill for each other," he said, letting the words drop like stones.

"No, there must be some mistake. Some crazy coincidence. Tom couldn't, he wouldn't..."

"Come now, Mrs Parker. I think that we are having established that there are many things which you do not know about your husband and I can be helping to fill some of the blanks. Here are the facts; your husband was part of this gang. Not just part of it, but very big man in the gang with lots of killings to his name."

I lay there, waiting to wake up from this nightmare. To be shaken awake by those caring hands. I closed my eyes and let a single, sparkling tear roll down my face and splash on to the dusty, concrete floor, amongst the dirt and ash, its purity destroyed as soon as it left my cheek. My mind was racing as I tried to look back on our life together and piece together some clues, to gather evidence in defence of Tom, even if it was just so that I could deliver a not guilty verdict in my mind and lay him to rest in my heart.

My mind combed through numerous recollections of Tom like someone quickly flipping through a photo album in search of a long forgotten print. It settled on a memory after we had been together for about six months.

It was a chilly evening in May and Tom was walking me

home after dinner at Lazio's Italian Restaurant, his long coat draped around my shoulders. We were both in high spirits from a great night and also the numerous glasses of red wine which we had knocked back, leaving me with that warm and fuzzy feeling, as if nothing else in the world mattered apart from the two of us in that perfect moment. I stopped and nestled my head into Tom's chest, closing my eyes as I did so, a dopey grin on my face.

"Hey little miss sleepy, no time for snoozing now. We got to get you home. You may be skinny but I'm not carrying you all the way," he said as he placed his strong arms around me, pulling me into him.

"I'm not snoozing, just enjoying the moment," I slurred, as I snuggled in closer to his chest, sleep beginning to drift over me.

"But you forgot your camera! How can you enjoy a moment without it!" he teased, laughing and kissing the top of my head.

"Cheeky!" I said, slapping him playfully on the arm. "Although it would make a beautiful picture," I mused, dozily looking up at him and smiling.

"Well, you do look kind of hot in my big coat all the way down to your knees. Especially with those big puffy sleep eyes. Maybe we should have brought the camera," he said, smiling again. I looked down at myself and realised how bad I must have looked.

"Oh no. I bet I look awful. Come on, let's get home," I said running a hand through my dishevelled hair, then pulling the coat tighter around me as the cool air nipped at my reddened cheeks.

"You may look a mess, but," he said, pausing for effect, "I still love you." Suddenly I was jolted awake from the alcoholic blur. Despite such a fairy-tale few months, Tom never said those magic words which meant so much to me. After about our third date I had blurted them out, then wished I could have drawn them back when I saw the panic in his eyes. Inwardly I cursed, fearing I may have scared him off, and so I vowed not to say them again until he did, worrying that I may never hear them from his mouth. But now here he was, freely saying those words I so wanted to hear. I took a step back, holding his arms as I did so and looked up so that I could see his whole face.

"What did you just say?" I asked, my eyes sparkling.

"I said, Rachel Imogen Cooper, I am head over heels in love with you. You are the only good thing I have in my life and I am determined not to mess this up. Even with your puffy eyes and gentleman's coat you look stunning to me and I never want to lose you. I need you more than you know," he said, squeezing my hands as the tears rolled down my cheeks. "I love you," he whispered, taking my hand and kissing it.

Although we had spent an amazing few months together I had never heard Tom speak like this, to be so open. He was always so restrained when it came to expressing emotions and I always felt like there was an untapped ocean of his feelings lying beneath the surface. I didn't know or care if it was the wine bringing it out, all that mattered was that he loved me. He pulled me close and kissed me hard on the lips, my salty tears rubbing on his cheeks. We parted and I smiled back at him, my heart feeling like it was on fire.

"Say it again," I whispered, giggling giddily.

"I said, I love you. I love you, I love you," shouting the words a little louder each time until he was screaming the words, 'I love you' on the bustling street, his arms flung wide like a character in an old black and white film.

I stood with a huge grin on my face, glowing red from mild embarrassment, the wine and the deep joy inside.

At that moment a group of three lads were swaggering by. Hearing Tom, one of them with an obvious fake tan, bleached hair and pint glass in hand stopped and eyed me up and down.

"If that's true mate, I wouldn't shout about it. She's a munter," he spat out, looking to his friends for acknowledgement. They all laughed, slapping him on the back and spilling their pints as they did so, beginning to walk off down the street.

"What did you just say?" Tom growled at the back of the

kid with the bleached hair. His mate turned round, equally orange and with spiky black hair. He replied,

"What's up mate, you deaf as well as blind? "'e said that your bird was a munter. You got a problem with that?"

I could feel every single muscle in Tom's body tense as I lay my hand on his arm.

"Tom, leave it, they're just a bunch of kids. It's not worth it," I said softly to him.

"Yeah, just you listen to your lady and trot on home now," the third one with a shaved head chipped in, waving his hand dismissively at us. "It's not worth it," he said in a high pitched voice clearly trying to imitate me, his friends falling about in laughter and also repeating it in ludicrous voices. They turned to walk off, Blondie casually tossing his pint glass at our feet as they left, spraying the pavement with shards of glass.

Before I could utter a word, Tom had landed a punch on the back of Blondie's head, knocking him to the floor. The other two had turned in shock and Tom punched Spikey square in the face, his nose looking like it had exploded as blood sprayed on to his white shirt. The third one swung for Tom, but with little power owing to his alcohol consumption. Tom ducked, then punched him in the stomach, doubling him over. As he gasped for breath Tom brought his knee in to Baldy's face. He toppled over and landed on the ground as Tom kicked him hard in the ribs. Then again and again, like a machine bent only on destruction. Cries rang out from the boy whose earlier bravado had now disappeared, and he looked more like a helpless child. A small crowd of drinkers from the pub over the road had come outside to watch and jeer, all keeping a safe distance. A few were talking animatedly on phones, no doubt calling the police.

I screamed out to Tom to stop, but he rhythmically continued to kick the boy as the other two remained on the ground. I ran over and grabbed him around the shoulders trying to pull him back. He spun around and raised his fist to strike then looked at me with eyes I had never seen before, clouded with rage. Slowly recognition spread across his frenzied face. He froze for a moment, then looked at his hand, clenched in a fist, ready to strike. He brought it down and placed it on my shoulder. I flinched and took a step back, my face contorted with shock.

"Rachel, I would never hurt you," he said, trying to regain his breathing. I shook my head and began to back away. "This was to protect you," he said, his face like that of a confused child who has been scolded when he was only trying to help. "Rachel?" He asked as I continued to back away.

"Tom, we will talk about this later. Right now, we have to get out of here," I hissed, gesturing with my eyes to the crowd of onlookers who were beginning to make their way over the road towards us.

The foreboding sound of sirens rang out in the distance as we hurriedly turned to leave.

# Chapter Eight

*Eventually I managed to heave myself from the flooded gutter, the road awash with rubbish and excrement. I headed back towards the market desperately hoping that someone there would be able to put me on the first step on my path back to Aisha. I frantically traced back over the route we had run trying to think of any kind of clue as to why someone would have taken my beautiful daughter but found nothing as I scanned the deserted streets. Compared to the usual vitality and life it felt like a seaside town shut down for winter as the rain continued to lash down.*

*I arrived back at the bustling market, people buying, selling and haggling. All appeared completely oblivious to everything that had just happened. Stalls we had cut through and things we had knocked over were rebuilt as if nothing had occurred moments earlier. I urgently approached people, quickly asking what they had seen and what they knew. All that I met though were turned down eyes and shakes of the head. These people who were always so warm and engaging seemed to have taken a vow of silence, their eyes filled with fear as I approached. "Kuch nahi," they muttered, "I know nothing". Even those people who I regarded as friends, people we spoke to most days gave the same sullen faces and denials. I pressed them, shook them, pleaded, cried, offered* money, but none of these brought even the slightest detail on what had happened or who had taken my beautiful daughter.

People moved as they saw me approaching, the reaction given to lepers and the insane. Pity and shame reflected in the eyes of those who dared glance at me, leaving me to feel like everyone was privy to a dirty secret I wasn't allowed to know.

Just as I had given up all hope of answers, I felt a bunch of frail fingers tighten on my wrist amongst the crowd and the words, "Saiful Das," whispered into my ear. The hand loosened and an old beggar I recognised from Park Street shuffled off through the crowd without another word.

I pushed through the busy market place after him, knocking people out of the way in my hurry as I called for him to stop. He pushed on, increasing his pace as people turned to stare at us both. As I caught up I grabbed his shoulder and spun him around, wildly asking in Hindi what saifuldas meant. His eyes filled with fear as a crowd began to gather and stare and he shook his head, pulling away from me. "Kuch nahi," he said to every question I asked, backing away into the crowd. I followed, pulling all the rupees from my pocket and pressing them against his chest. He held his hooked hand in the air, letting the notes fly off into the breeze. This caused a commotion, everyone diving wildly to grab the money. Amidst the movement he slipped away and despite trying to give chase, he was nowhere to be seen.

*Hurriedly I began to ask those in the crowd what saifuldas was, but was met with the same blank faces as people moved away from me. I repeated the word over and over to myself, trying to figure out its meaning. Saifuldas, saifuldas, saiful das, Saiful Das! It must be a name. I had taught numerous children with the surname Das, though I had never encountered anyone with the name Saiful.*

*Regardless of any further information, I now had a name, a sign post directing me on the road back to Aisha, although the sign post gave no indication of how long the journey would be, nor all that would be required to complete that journey.*

*I wrestled with the idea of contacting the police, fearing that their involvement may have hampered my plans for revenge once I had found Aisha. Also, the tales of corruption I had heard and the stories within the school of the bribery certain teachers had faced at the hands of the police made me wary but I felt there was a greater possibility of finding her with the Indian police force rather than me searching alone.*

*I headed home and found the most recent photo I had of Aisha, one in which she wore a bright pink salwar kameez with sequins which sparkled when she moved. I also raided my drawers for any rupees which I had, remembering my previous encounters with the police where bakshee or bribery was the common currency. It seemed that a little money went a long way in making yourself innocent in the eyes of the law here and that anything could be forgotten for a few hundred rupees. I just hoped that for a few thousand my daughter could be found.*

*As I entered the Police Station I was approached by a very stern looking officer with a rifle slung over his shoulder. He looked me up and down then asked what I wanted. I began to explain that my daughter had been taken and showed him a photo of Aisha. This prompted a number of questions about if she was really my daughter, who the mother was, where her mother was now and why had I not reported her disappearance to the police. I was led into a small, sweltering room for questioning and made to sit and wait amongst the piles of paperwork which filled the shelves from floor to ceiling. It took at least forty minutes and several complaints from me before three officers arrived, all beginning again to ask the same questions about Aisha and Layla, one of them scribbling furiously while the others looked at me with suspicion.*

*I was hot, tired, frustrated and becoming incoherent as I had to relive the painful past of Layla's disappearance knowing that every second wasted talking about this was a second closer to Aisha being gone forever. I shouted these exact thoughts at the officers present and stood to leave. The shorter of the pair questioning me, who I later learned was* called Superintendent Roy moved to block the way. Sucking on his cigarette he informed me, "Mr Parker, I would not be doing that. At the moment you are getting yourself in trouble with missing wife and daughter. It appears you have been very careless to be losing both. We must be looking in to this before we start looking for these criminals which you are speaking about. How do we know it was not you who made them disappear? You must be giving us some evidence of this," he said, blowing smoke in my face.

"What kind of evidence? I've come here to report my daughter disappearing. Why would I do that if I had her?" I asked, perplexed.

"Evidence, hmmm. I think about ek lakh, one hundred thousand rupees, should convince us of your innocence and maybe another ek lakh could convince us to start looking in to where your daughter has gone," he said with a wry smile on his face.

"This is outrageous!" I yelled you are supposed to help people, not blackmail them!

Roy looked at me, a wry smile playing on his face. "Well Mr Parker, what will you do? Tell the police!" he said, his smile widening to reveal his yellowed teeth. "If you are not paying you are not leaving, now sit down please, Mr Parker."

I kicked the chair across the room then looked at Roy, waving my finger inches from his face. "My daughter is out *there, taken who knows where and you want to try and arrest me for reporting her missing? This is an absolute joke," I said, my body shaking with rage. The other two officers moved swiftly, one approaching from each side to take my arms and restrain me, but Roy motioned with his hand for them to leave me.*

*"We could always be adding assault on a police officer to kidnap of a wife and child," he said, goading me to strike out "You will be liking your time spent here, very lovely prisons... unless," he said, rubbing his fingers and thumb together in the international money symbol. "We will be giving you time to think things over." He turned to face the door, the other two officers following him like shadows.*

*"OK, OK," I shouted, realising the helplessness of my situation. I rummaged in my bag and pulled out the money I had scraped together before I left the apartment. It was just short of twenty thousand rupees. "Look, this is all that I have got. Please. I just want my daughter back," I said throwing the notes on the table. Roy tilted his head to one of the other men who promptly swept the notes into a bag he had ready.*

*"Your care for your daughter is very touching. In fact, I am thinking you are successful in convincing me that it was not in fact you who was taking her away. Now..." he motioned to the guy with the note pad who resumed his primary position, "if you would be so good as to tell us from the start*

what happened, we will be doing our absolute best to be helping you," he said, smiling broadly.

I clenched my jaws and breathed deeply through my nose trying to regain my composure. As furious as it made me, I knew that if I left now my chances of finding Aisha would be close to zero. With these flawed officers as my only option my chances were probably only slightly higher but I rationalised that they may serve some use.

"She was taken this morning in the market place just off Tollygunge by some guy called Saiful Das," I said. At this the scribbler stopped writing and all three men glanced nervously at each other, the atmosphere suddenly changing. It was as if a magic word had been spoken.

"Saiful Das? How are you knowing this information? You were seeing him?" Roy asked, drawing very heavily on his cigarette.

"No, I have no idea who he is or what he looks like but some guy told me that it was him. Why, who is he?" I asked.

"He is a man who makes this finding your daughter a lot more dangerous. Tell me, who is this man that told you about Das?" he asked, looking nervously at me.

"I don't know his name. He's a beggar. He's always sitting on the corner near the Tollygunge market. He only has one arm and he's got a big ginger beard." Roy tilted his head in recognition.

*"And he would swear that it was Das? He was being sure about this," he said, looking me in the eye.*

*"Yeah, he came and told me who it was in the market place, if not I would have no idea who it was that had taken her," I confessed.*

*"Well then, it is very good of him to have given this information. I am sure he will be rewarded," Roy said, motioning for the Officer without the paper and pen to exit which he did without looking back. However, the door had no sooner closed than it was flung open again by an older officer with silver hair and round glasses looking slightly like a blustered owl. His skin was very dark and his face pitted and scarred. Under his arms were numerous files with paper falling out of them and in his spare hand he carried a steaming glass cup of chai. Roy's jaw clenched as the man plonked the chai on the table in front of me and extended his free hand.*

*"Mr Parker, I am so sorry to have kept you waiting. I am Senior Superintendent Dipal and I will be helping you find your daughter. This is a terrible business. I hope my colleagues have been, ah, helpful? But I am afraid they will be leaving us now," he said, the last part delivered to Roy, his contempt thinly veiled. Roy began to open his mouth in protest, before Dipal growled something too rapidly in Hindi for me to understand. Roy nodded to the other Officer and*

*they both slowly left the room, Roy's eyes fixed on Dipal, his pockets stuffed with my rupees. Dipal watched the door close, his eyes full of fire. As he turned to me that flame diffused and he broke into an apologetic smile. "Very sorry about that sir, I do not want you to be thinking that I am wasting your time giving your account to so many different officers. I will be taking full charge on this case and as Senior Superintendent you will be given my full attention." As he spoke he walked over to the fan in the corner of the room turning it on and moving it in my direction to provide some relief from the heat.*

*"Now please, if you could be telling me everything which has happened and we will be seeing if it is possible to find your daughter."*

*My confusion and irritation at the time which was being wasted was partly diffused by the genuine apology and concern radiating from Dipal. His kind eyes seemed to empathise with my pain rather than seeing it as something to cash in on. I still expected to be asked for what seemed to be the standard bakshee but none was requested as I gave Dipal the most detailed account I could of what had happened that day. He nodded gravely as I once more explained the events and again nodded his head when I mentioned the name Saiful Das, rubbing his tired eyes with his hands. He looked up at me, his face creased and grey, and released a long sighed.*

*"Who is this Saiful Das? What's going to happen to my*

*little girl?" I pleaded.*

*"I am afraid Mr Parker that is not a simple answer. There are a number of different things which may have happened. First of all we need to be sure that it was Saiful Das, which I have little reason to doubt, but if it is finding your daughter will be very difficult. Saiful Das is the head of the most organised people trafficking gang in Kolkata and in all honesty, probably the whole of India. He is very organised making it very difficult to see any allegations count against him. People can be taken and made to disappear, removed from Kolkata and shipped to Mumbai, Nepal or even England and probably ninety nine per cent of them are never seen again. They can be gone like that," he said, clicking his fingers, "as can any witnesses who stand up against him," he said through gritted teeth.*

*"Ninety nine per cent!" I exclaimed, placing my head in my hands as my heart dropped. "How many people are taken every year?"*

*"It is impossible to be accurate. There are hundreds of thousands every year although that is only those we have reported. There are probably three times that number which are not reported, maybe more," he said gravely.*

*"Why would people not report their kids being stolen?" I asked, baffled that someone would not report such a horrendous thing.*

*Dipal sighed, and again rubbed his bloodshot eyes. "Many reasons. Sadly, due to people such as Superintendent Roy who you met earlier we are not always seen as the force for good which we aim to be. Truth always prevails," he said, pointing to the badge he had on his brown Police shirt. "That is our motto which seems to have been forgotten by many in this department. Because of that some are just too scared to be able to come and speak to us, some fear that they will be extorted. Also, around ninety percent of those taken are from the Dalit caste."*

*I looked at him blankly. "What are the Dalit caste?" I asked. He ran his fingers through his bushy mane of white hair and sighed.*

*"You are aware of the caste system here in India?"*

*I knew very little so again I shook my head. He thought for a moment and then began to speak.*

*"This is something which it is important for you to know so that you can understand how Das operates. There is so much to cover here, but I will paint for you with very broad strokes. Basically, Indian society was divided up many, many years ago into four different castes or groups as you would call them,' he said, hurriedly looking around his desk and picking up an apple, a small note book, two rulers and two small erasers and hastily arranged them into an ad-lib body. "These four groups were to represent the body of Brahman, or God,*

*the Supreme Being. Here at the top," he said, picking up the apple for emphasis, "is the head. The knowledge, the elite. Those falling into this group are known as Brahmins and they are held with the utmost respect in society. These people are your Priests, teachers, scholars. They are the social elite, revered by followers of Hinduism and what they say is what happens. Obviously after thousands of years at the top of this social pyramid they are in no hurry to relinquish their power."*

*I nodded impatiently and sipped my chai, trying to figure out how this linked to Aisha being taken. Dipal took the hint and began to speak more hurriedly.*

*"Next in the social order is the group known as the Kshatriyas," he said, laying his hand on the notebook as a makeshift torso. "These were kings, warriors, those who enforce the law and people such as administrators. This is the group which generally enjoy the majority of political power. Next," he said, quickly pulling up the two rulers and holding them up for me to see, "are the legs of Brahman. This group are known as the Vaishyas. These often have quite a lot of economic power and were merchants or traders. Those dealing in business, traders, bankers, land owners. In many ways they now hold most power in society as the rupee becomes the new god to too many. And finally," he placed the rulers back and picked up the two erasers which had been*

*used to mark the feet. "The Shudras. Craftsmen. Labourers. Those who tend to do the physical, manual labour and obviously being at the bottom of the pyramid there are a huge number of this group." He leaned back in his chair and sighed. "There we have a brief introduction to the caste system in all its glory. Everyone has their place and everyone knows their role. What your family do, you then do. You work in that caste, socialise in that caste, marry in that caste and are eventually buried according to your caste. Everyone stays in their group so that there are enough people in each role or so the thinking goes," he said with disdain.*

*"Ok," I said, "but what has this got to do with us finding my daughter?" He held up a placating hand.*

*"Well, the reason for which I have told you all this is because of a final group within this caste system, or technically I should say outside the caste system. Here in India this group number around two hundred and fifty million and are known as the Dalits or the Untouchables, because, as the name suggests, no one will touch them. This group are not recognised as even being part of Brahma and therefore they are not treated as human. In some ways they are regarded as being lower than animals, all because of the caste they are born into. In the villages many are not even permitted to enter a police station. As soon as they are born all they can do is sweep the streets or clean others toilets. There have been*

*rules brought in to try and even things out, reserving a number of jobs for the Dalits in Government and Official roles, but there are not enough educated Dalits to fill these positions and it means these roles are left empty causing even more animosity towards them. The stigma they are born into makes their self-esteem so low, as do centuries of history that most feel they deserve to be treated in this way. Can you imagine that Mr Parker? Being born and raised to feel all you will amount to is cleaning up others shit?"*

*I shook my head and wondered how I had been so blissfully unaware of this rigid social division, just assuming the poor were poor and the rich were rich.*

*"I know this all too well myself. I was born to a Dalit family, a family of street sweepers, told by everyone I would be nothing. That this would be my life too. But I was stubborn. I had dreams and managed to escape that life, to travel to England, to learn your language. To study law and eventually get a reserved job through a law called the Mandal Commission here in the Police. Yet still, after all this travel and study and work I am not accepted here. I have a position but no respect. Mandal filth I am called, Dalit scum because of my name and the family I was born into."*

*I looked at him as he clenched and unclenched his fists.*

*"It is a tragedy and because of this, as you can imagine, most Dalits are trapped in poverty, most with no education,*

*no job prospects and no opportunity to see further than the day ahead. Some have eight, nine, ten children," he said, counting these off on his fingers. "No idea about family planning, some hoping that one child may bring them money and support the family but it is just another mouth to feed. Children are sent out to scavenge or beg and very often the parents are left with the difficult option of slowly watching all their children starve, or to sacrifice one for the rest. People like Saiful Das know this and prey on their weakness, sending an agent to speak to the family. The agent fills their head with promises for the child, how they will be taken care of, given a very good job and be able to support the whole family. They pay a pittance for the child and take them to another city, away from family, friends or any connections. Once they arrive they are told they now owe lots of money for the transport, any food along the way and for finding them the job. They now have a huge debt to work off and are put to work in horrendous jobs for long hours. Some are put into bonded labour, being forced to cook and clean in rich households for up to twenty hours a day. Others are taken and forced into begging. They are put to work for a gang who will go out begging, often given a baby and sometimes deliberately disfigured so people will have compassion and give them more money. Others are taken and used as prostitutes in one of many brothels."*

*As Dipal listed the horrendous possibilities I completely lost control and sat and wept, my shoulders heaving up and down as I sobbed, the consequences of what could happen to my little girl overwhelming. So beautiful, so innocent, how could someone deliberately take that away from her?*

*I punched the table in frustration and stood up, leaning against the wall and trying to steady my breathing. Dipal waited patiently, looking through his notes as I steadied myself. I turned around as he pulled out a faded black and white photo of a girl around ten.*

*"There is hope Mr Parker," he said as he patted the photo. "This is a girl called Sunita who lived in my village. She was born into a Dalit family and had a brother and a sister. Their father was an alcoholic who cared only where his next drink was coming from. One day he had the idea that it was now time for his children to be making him money so that he could do even less and drink even more. At the time, all three were lucky enough to be in a school run by an NGO charity, but he decided to pull the two girls out of there, leaving the boy in school as he thought one day he would get a good job that would bring in even more money. The father sold these girls to an agent, much the same as the way in which Das operates. Sunita was only ten and her sister, Ajita was twelve. He sold them for two thousand rupees each, not knowing or caring what would become of them. That night, when the boy*

*returned home he found his father drunk and asked where his sisters were. The father told him and he ran to the police for help but they would not even allow him in the station to file a report. The next day he went to the school and told the charity workers who promised to help. They spoke to the Police and after much pressure they agreed to help with the case. The charity paid for the investigation and after a few weeks they tracked both girls to a brothel in Mumbai after Sunita had managed to phone home and alert her brother of her whereabouts. Along with the Police they performed a raid, rescuing Sunita but Ajita had already been moved elsewhere. They continued searching but after a year nothing more was done and she was lost and never found again." He paused and looked down at his folded hands for a moment before continuing.*

*"It still haunts me that her sister was never rescued and that is what inspired me to become a police officer, to help people who had no choice in life. Having seen how slowly the police were to react that is why I did not want your case handled by extortionists like Roy who would have no interest in helping you." He paused and looked me in the eye. "I swear to move mountains to help you Mr Parker and I will not rest until we find your Aisha."*

*He stretched out his hand as a symbol of his sincerity and as we shook neither of us realised how many mountains would have to be moved and how difficult it would be to move them.*

*He handed me the photo of Sunita. "This is a symbol of hope Mr Parker and reminds me in the dark times that salvation is possible. Please, I want you to keep it safe till we find your Aisha."*

*I nodded and took the photo from Dipal, while handing him the photo of Aisha I had brought along. He held the photo close to his face then nodded.*

*"She is a beautiful child. What lovely emerald eyes," he said and tapped his pen against his teeth, pausing for a moment to think. "This is quite an unusual case, but it may be the peculiarity of it which gives us an advantage at finding Aisha. As I just explained, the majority of children trafficked are Dalits, many of these sold into it by their own family or else tricked. Now, there are a large number of gangs who are involved in this and the gang of Saiful Das is probably the most organised and notorious, closely followed by the rival gang of Chotu Pandney. Das is the mastermind behind most of it but will rarely be involved in the actual dirty work of taking the people or putting them to work. He is too clever to risk putting himself in that danger. Because of his strategising it is often impossible to trace the movement of one person to their destination as they may be taken by Das then sold to another group in Mumbai or a contact abroad. These people*

*are just seen as business packages which are milked for all the money they can bring in and are then discarded. He is a businessman who can see a profit and maybe this greed will be his downfall."*

*He paused again and subconsciously cracked his fingers. "I assume that Aisha had been watched for a while by Das and his gang. Knowing she was not a Dalit and having a gora father he would know bribery was not an option, so I assume that he saw kidnapping as the only viable option to take her as one of his... assets." He held the photo in front of him while continuing. "She is extremely beautiful and no doubt will be worth a huge amount to him, especially with her light skin and green eyes. However, this makes her unique and maybe easier to find. If I may, I would like to take this picture and show it to a number of contacts I have in the city who may be able to help?" I nodded.*

*"Please, try anything if you think it will work," I begged.*

*"Speed is the key Mr Parker," he said, raising a finger to make his point. "If she is not found by tonight I am afraid that our mission will become far more difficult," he stated darkly as he hastily gathered up the files from the table and gestured towards the door. "I will call as soon as we have any news. If not, please report back tomorrow morning and we will discuss the next course of action, but for now," he said, pointing to the picture of Sunita in my hand, "have hope."*

*I walked home, the photo of Sunita held tightly in my hand as I tried to block out the incessant thoughts of what may have happened to Aisha. I went back towards the market place to find the beggar who had directed me towards Das to thank him. As I approached all that greeted me was his makeshift cardboard home and his small bag of possessions. He was gone.*

## Chapter Nine

Had I somehow been so blinded by love that I had not seen that man who held me, kissed me and made me feel secure was actually a monstrous murderer? Had the signs been there all along but I had just been too deluded to see them? Surely even as smitten as I was I would have seen through a façade that grand? Surely?

I shuddered at the idea of Tom as a killer, trying to push away the grainy images of the dead bodies which Roy had shown me. This must be some elaborate coincidence. Roy must have his facts distorted. If only Tom were alive now to clarify it all, to explain the real series of events.

I sat, flicking my gaze between the three bodies displayed before me and the corpse of Tom a few feet away. Was he really linked to these men? Had he laughed with them, fought with them, *killed* with them? It was not possible, surely. That was not the man I knew. I thought back through our happy memories, trying to cleanse my mind of these sinister allegations, remembering him as joyful, loving and tender.

My mind alighted on one particularly beautiful evening from four years ago. I arrived home one night finding the door open. I entered cautiously into the dark, spotting a trail of candles leading me through the living room into the dining room. The smell of roasting lamb filled the house and a Norah

Jones melody accompanied my every step. I grinned, peeking into the kitchen expecting to see Tom busy at work, but the only sign of life was a few pots busily bubbling away. I followed the path of candles into the dining room, which led to a bunch of seven red roses laid in the middle of our plates on the table. I picked them up, inhaling their aroma and beamed in delight. Under them was a small note which read simply, "I love you for the light you bring to a dark place."

Holding the note in my hand I noticed that the candles continued winding their way down into my basement, a makeshift dark room I had constructed to process my prints. Intrigued, I followed, pushing the door gently open then shutting it quickly, blinking so my eyes could adjust to the light. As they came into focus in the soft red light I saw four pictures pegged to the drying line, a separate word photographed on each. WILL-YOU-MARRY-ME? I gasped, then screamed, clapping my hands together as I hopped from foot to foot, tears of joy sparkling down my cheeks. With a loud cough I suddenly became aware of Tom kneeling in front of me, an open box with a diamond ring sparkling in the dimmed red light.

"Rachel, you always talk about holding things in photos to keep them perfect, but to me, every day with you is a bit more perfect than the last. You're amazing. I love you. Basically, what I'm trying to say is, well, will you? Will you be my wife?" he said, raising the box towards me.

I yelped again. "Yes! Yes! Yes!" I shouted, unable to communicate any more than that as Tom slid the ring onto my finger.

He took my hands, then pulled me into an embrace as we waltzed in the limited space between washing lines. I nuzzled my head into his shoulder, and then looked into his smiling face, seeing the man with whom I wanted to grow old, learning to love a little more each moment.

"I love you," I whispered. Suddenly his face distorted and his hands fell from mine. "What's wrong?" I asked fearfully, my emotions already haywire.

"I forgot the bloody potatoes!" he exclaimed, turning and running up the stairs.

The next morning I awoke in a hazy state of bliss, rolling over to hold Tom, but on his creased pillow lay a hurried note. I wondered if it was to be a new inventive surprise for how to spend the day but its content woke me with a start.


*Rachel,*

*I cannot put into words how much I love you. I would be with you forever if it was possible but I fear that I have made so many mistakes that I don't deserve you. My heart is deeply scarred and I fear that I will not be able to be who you need me to be. I have made so many mistakes and it is unfair for you to be yoked to me for a lifetime. I am leaving in the hope that I may save you from myself. I am more sorry than you will ever know.*

*All my love,*

*Tom*

I leapt out of bed, shouting Tom's name all over the house but he was gone. Hurriedly I pulled on my tracksuit bottoms, a coat and hat and headed to his house hoping with all my strength that he would still be there. As I arrived he was sat outside the door looking dishevelled, one small suitcase in his hand.

I charged up to him, letter in hand and thumped it into his chest. Then I punched him again and again, pounding my fists into his body as he absorbed the blows, not even raising a hand in defence. Eventually, when I was too exhausted to keep punching I held the note up in front of him, shaking, and shouted, "why? How can you just propose then run out on me? I thought you loved me! Were you just going to run away?" I said, disgustedly pointing to his suitcase.

"Rachel, I love you so much and that's why I have to go. There's so much in here," he said, pointing to his heart, "that it's not fair for you to put up with it. I've done so much wrong. Kept so much from you that is unforgivable. When I was younger..."

"We all have," I shouted, cutting him off. "Tom, we all mess up, I don't care about your past. All I care about is who you are now and who you will be as my husband." He slowly shook his head, looking at the ground.

"It's not fair on you. There are so many things that I can't ask you to deal with."

"Well let me decide that! I will gladly deal with it if it means I can be with you," I said, laying my arm on his shoulder. He shrugged it off.

"I shouldn't have let you get so close. I didn't mean to hurt you," he mumbled, putting his hands in his pockets.

"Well don't hurt me then. Marry me! I love you for who you are, perfect or not," I said gently grabbing the front of his shirt.

"There are so many mistakes though in my past. So much I have done wrong."

"That was the past. It doesn't matter anymore!"

"But I was..." he began.

"Was! I don't care about was! I love you just as you are you big ass!" I shouted, shaking him as I spoke. "Now will you please just put that case back?"

He opened his mouth to reply, then nodded bashfully. I grabbed his head tightly in both my hands and pulled it towards me. "Don't ever think about running off and leaving me."

"I won't," he vowed, then picked me up in his arms. "I am yours forever."

Sitting here now, his silent body next to me and wild accusations flying I wish that I had actually heard the past from Tom's own lips. What were the confessions which he had wished to make?

## Chapter Ten

*I walked over to the space on the cracked pavement the beggar had claimed as his own with his tattered mat and makeshift tarpaulin covering held by two shaky bamboo sticks. On it rested one hemp bag with all of his possessions in the world scattered in the street for everyone to see. His single change of tattered shirt, a metal cup, a key ring of the goddess Lakshmi and a used yellowed bandage. An odd assortment, but all the possessions he had managed to gather in his life filled with struggle which were now carelessly tossed aside by whoever had taken him. Whatever had happened to him was completely my fault. I had brought this fate on him.*

*I delicately placed the items back inside the bag and left it neatly on the corner of his threadbare mat. Laying my hand on the bag and murmuring a short prayer for him, I feared this may have been his only burial service. Before rising I whispered my apologies to his now sacred spot and asked for his forgiveness for the danger I had recklessly placed him in.*

*I left there and quickly started walking to try and distance myself from the guilt in my heart, but still it remained. I stumbled through the whole night, too exhausted to sleep, remorse and fear holding me prisoner. Every corner I turned felt like I was suddenly seeing things with new eyes. On arrival to Kolkata my heart had been stirred every time I saw a child begging but after a few months it had just become a regular occurrence and to be honest, it shames me to tell you, a bit of a nuisance. Now though it felt as if I were a raw bag of nerves, the sight of every abandoned child making me want to weep.*

*I felt a small hand slip inside mine as I marched along and my heart leapt, but as I looked down there was a small boy with shaggy hair, his eyes boring into my soul as he repeated 'uncle, uncle' over and over and motioned with his hand to his mouth for food. I crouched down and held his face gently in front of me seeing only Aisha and imagining this vagrant life for her. Instinctively I pulled him in to me for a hug, his bony body rattling as I convulsed with sobs. His expression changed to confusion as he held out his hand for money and rubbed his belly, pushing me away with the other hand. I placed twenty rupees in his hand and watched as his confusion turned to glee while he tucked the note into his pocket before sprinting off, a huge smile on his dirty face.*

*I sat down on the pavement and watched as other children surrounded him and shouted merrily. Sleepily I looked around, unaware of which part of the city I had stumbled into. Night was falling and all around me families were simply lying down on the hard street for their beds. Some had ingeniously designed small homes using old hessian sacks, planks of wood and any other materials they were able to scavenge. Others had cardboard to cushion the hard floor while most were left with only the pavement as their mattress.*

*As I sat and observed the nightly customs, five of the children surrounding the boy I had given the money to honed in towards me like sharks smelling blood. They ran over to me shouting and hollering as I began to get to my feet. All adopted the same pout as the boy before, gesticulating to their mouths for food and repeating, "uncle, uncle", as they jostled to get closest to me. One girl of about seven was holding an infant in her arms and had a black patch over one eye. Another boy had only a stump for one arm and rubbed it, his eyes pleading. These were all familiar sights on the streets of Kolkata, things I had seen thousands of times before, but tonight I was seeing them for the first time since my arrival with the empathy that they deserve. There was a tragic story behind each child and the wasted life they were forced into. I wondered if these children had only ever known the squalor in which they lived or if life had promised more for them like it had my Aisha. These kids were not just a charity photo opportunity but real people with real stories. When the day finished they had literally nothing to eat and even that had to be shared. I regretted that it had taken the thought that my daughter may have been among them to break my apathy.*

*Pleading, I held up a photo of Aisha to them and asked in*

*broken Hindi if they had seen her. They all clambered towards the picture for a better look, knocking each other out of the way in the process. The girl at the front shouted, 'bu-yu-tee-ful,' in an attempt at English. I asked again if they had seen her, but heads were shaken and then the gestures resumed for food. I pulled the last few rupees in change I had and handed them to the bigger girl who was at the front of the crowd. I gestured for her to share and she nodded eagerly. As they walked off I saw the girl counting the money and dividing the spoils between each member of the group, like a mother doling out pocket money to her children.*

*I looked down and standing patiently was a girl of about six looking up at me, her eyes sparkling and seeming to shine in contrast to her tattered dress. I tried to explain that I had no money but she shook her head then pointed to the original boy I had given the money to. I looked quizzically at her then she wrapped her arms around my leg in a hug for a few seconds before running back to the rest of the group. I smiled as the tears fell, then turned and began to trudge slowly back up the street in hope of regaining my bearings.*

*I pounded the streets for the entire night, photo in hand, showing it to anyone who was awake and would listen. I was pointed one way then the other, many promising that they could find her for only fifty rupees. I was treated with suspicion, pity and contempt. I felt hope then despair. I walked and ran, whispered and shouted but all of it was to no avail. It felt as if my hope was measured in an hour glass and that every grain of sand falling was a grain of hope disappearing forever. By sunrise it felt as if the glass was almost empty.*

*As the first rays of sun appeared I made my way to the Police Station hoping that Dipal had received better luck than me, but one look at his grey, hapless face told me all I needed to know. His eyes were bloodshot and puffy, his hair now even more ruffled and his cheek creased like a sheet of paper tossed in the waste. He looked at me and slowly shook his head.*

*"Your daughter is gone Mr Parker," he said in an unnaturally loud voice, almost as if he were an actor on stage, projecting his words. A number of officers stopped typing and looked up at the commotion. "I have looked everywhere and it is no good. She is lost to the streets. There is nothing more I can do for you. This case is closed I am afraid. I can waste no more time on your demands. Here is your picture," he said pressing the print I had given him of Aisha firmly against my chest. "Take this and leave, there is not another thing to be done. I am sorry for your loss. Good day," he said, not once making eye contact, then disappearing before I could ask a single detail of his search.*

*The typing remained on pause as I stood there bewildered,*

*my mouth opening and closing in disbelief as I watched Dipal slam his office door with a note of finality. What had happened to his promises? 'I won't stop until I find her,' I muttered bitterly, slowly shaking my head in disbelief. No wonder Sunita's sister was never found if this was all the effort put in. What a joke. Every eye was still watching me with intrigue as I slowly began to clap. "Great job guys, thanks! Couldn't have done it without you. Thanks for a sterling effort. Really, you should be proud," I said, exasperation getting the better of me. I turned on my heel, kicked a waste paper bin across the room then stormed out of the Station, a sea of silent eyes moving as one to accompany me to the exit.*

*Dipal had failed to find Aisha and I had now lost his support and expertise too. How had he become so dismissive after his bravado yesterday? I sat and looked at the picture of Aisha he had handed me and kissed her forehead. I traced my finger over her face, lost in thought about what I could do now having been deserted by my one and only ally. As my finger caressed its surface I felt raised lines running through her picture. I flipped it over and on the back was a note, scribbled in precise handwriting which read –*

***Mr Parker, I have made discoveries about your daughter. It is no longer safe to talk here. Meet me by the Kali temple in Kalighat as soon as possible. Dipal***

*I sprung to my feet and glanced nervously around as if it would be possible to see why it was no longer safe to talk, then stuffed the picture in my wallet, hurriedly departing from the Police Station. On reaching the Metro I retrieved the photo and re-read the short letter several times trying to glean any sub text or clues it offered about Aisha, but could not divine any deeper meaning that what was before me in black and white. However, the dying embers of the fire of hope stirred within me again as I travelled to Kalighat, nervous energy keeping my exhausted body alert.*

*I had never ventured to this part of the city before but as soon as I arrived the giant form of the Kali temple loomed over me, its white walls bold in the morning sun. The area outside was heaving with people, bustling back and forth. Beggars sat and chanted in the street and holy men and worshippers wandered in and out of the temple, some with blood daubed on their forehead. Numerous men had varying sizes of clay sculptures of the goddess Kali, dark in form with a bright red tongue protruding from her lips as she held a severed head in one hand and boasted a necklace made of them around her neck.*

*As I stared at the disturbing statue a claw like hand gripped on to my wrist and an old man with no teeth looked up at me, his eyes shrivelled like raisins. "Kali Goddess, goddess to death," he rasped, his head wobbling from side to side. "Puja, paanch rupees," he stated, holding up five digits for the amount of money he wanted while trying to pull me towards the temple. I shook my head and tried to pull my arm from his talons, but he held firm, fixing me with his dark eyes. "You. Destruction. Death. All around you. Must make puja to Kali," he said, punctuating every word by jabbing a finger at my heart.*

*Suddenly, a firm arm clamped down on my other shoulder causing me to gasp and a familiar voice shouted at the old man in Hindi. The old man sucked his gums then spat, walking off in the other direction, like a rabid dog. Holding me in a vice like grip was Dipal, dressed in a blue Punjabi suit adorned with a cap and shades. He pressed a finger to my lips, forbidding me to speak and dragged me through the crowd to a small shaded area away from the holy revellers. He ushered me in, casting a wary eye over the temple crowd and a group of white Europeans standing by a cart supping from a green coconut.*

*Now that I noticed it, this area seemed to be swarming in white Europeans and Americans. After being treated as a novelty item for my skin colour, there was probably a ratio of half Western tourists to the Indian nationals in this area. I was unsure why, but deduced that Dipal probably chose this area to make me appear less conspicuous as I rather obviously stood out everywhere else in the city.*

*I looked at Dipal, eagerly trying to search his face for answers, but the shades prevented me reading him. "What did you discover? Have you found her?" I whispered excitedly, clutching his arm. He slowly drew down the shades and shook his head, his face ashen and sunken.*

*"I am sorry if I have raised your hopes Mr Parker. I spent all of last night talking to contacts and asking about Aisha. After no small amount of bakshee I was able to gather some information which may prove useful to us, but I am afraid it was the news I feared." He rubbed his eyes and delivered the following information looking up towards the sky rather than at me. "Aisha was taken by Das, that is a certainty. She has been taken and sent to work within one of the brothels which he owns. She will not be set to work there yet though, not until she is older, but she will be given cleaning tasks and will run errands until she is old enough to..." he tailed off mid-sentence, making the implications very clear.*

*"I'm going to kill him. I'm going to rip that bastard's head clean off," I screamed, standing, to show my intent. Dipal leapt to his feet and pinned both my arms at my side.*

*"Maybe that opportunity will present itself, but right now, if you are to have a chance of finding your daughter you must sit down, be quiet and draw no attention to yourself," he hissed.*

*"How can I be calm if he is out there, pimping out my*

*daughter?" I said, taking all my energy to keep my voice from rising.*

*"You must. For her sake. If you lose it now, you will lose her for sure. Now sit down and listen to what we are going to do," Dipal commanded.*

*I breathed deeply and unclenched my fists, taking a seat again in the shade.*

*"Here are the facts. We know that she is alive. We know that she is with Das. We know that he has selected her for brothel work. We know, at the moment, that she is still in India and it is my guess that she will be kept here until she is older. These are the facts we can work with. However, as I mentioned, he is a big business man and has cast his net wide for larger returns. Therefore, she may well be anywhere in any brothel in India. We are not able to knock on the door of every brothel and even if we did, she would be hidden like that," he said, clicking his fingers, "and moved to a new location. This is why we must be smart, Mr Parker. From the outside, as we are, your daughter is lost. I have seen many cases all end the same way. There is only one way which I think we may succeed in reuniting you with your daughter." He looked at me sadly and sighed deeply.*

*"What is it? I will do anything to get her back," I growled.*

*"I was afraid you would say that Mr Parker." He rubbed his eyes again and pushed his hand through his hair,*

searching for the right words. *"Imagine if you were to try and capture a fortified city on a hill. It would have many armed soldiers, there would be hundreds against you. To break in is impossible. But, if you approach that city as a friend, once you are welcomed inside you may discover the weak spots, where the treasure is hidden and how you may take it without even being seen or suspected."*

*I raised my eyebrows in confusion, unsure what this talk of cities had to do with rescuing Aisha.*

*"You must join the gang," Dipal bluntly stated.*

*"Join the gang?" I almost screamed, "you mean, actually become part of this messed up group of child stealers?" He nodded silently.*

*"Well, how am I supposed to do that? If you hadn't noticed, I don't spend my free time buying and selling kids! How am I meant to just turn up and join? I doubt it's the same as the boy scouts!"*

*"Mr Parker, if you have a better idea, please, share it now. If not, shut up and listen. I do not have much time here and I fear we may already be in danger of drawing more than enough attention to ourselves. Now, I feared this may be the only option which is why I arranged to meet you here. If I had not spoken with you in the manner I did in the station people would assume we were still working together. This would lead to questions making it impossible for you to go under cover as*

*Das has ears even within the police station, which lead to wagging tongues if there is enough money for the information. For many, the police wages is just the cream on top of the money they make from people like Das." He raised a finger to my face, the intensity in his eyes frightening. "No-one must know we are in contact or your life will be in even more danger than your daughters. If we are to do this there is no going back. If you agree, I will help make the necessary arrangements, but who you are, your whole identity at this moment will be lost. Everything which you once were will be gone and one tiny little error will lead to a very unpleasant death. Can you accept that Mr Parker or do you wish to back out?" He held me in his steely gaze.*

*I hesitated for a moment then held out my hand to him. "I'm in. Nothing matters but getting her back." He shook my hand and nodded.*

*"Now, if you are within the gang and you can get close enough to Das you may be able to track Aisha down. He may have records of where girls go, you may be able to speak to other girls to track her. Who knows? But it will be a lot easier than being on the outside. And if you are able to get close enough to see how the whole operation works," he said, pulling at a cord on his sleeve, "you may help me to unravel this whole gang," he continued, giving it a tug. "Then we can destroy them the way they have destroyed so many others*

*lives," he said, punching his fist into his palm.*

*"So, how exactly am I going to get in to this gang and get close to Das?" I asked, my heart pumping twice its normal rate as the insanity of what I was proposing to do began to sink in.*

*"You have to be useful to him otherwise there is no point. You have to play to your assets. What makes you different to everyone else in the gang here?" he asked.*

*"I'm not sick and twisted? I don't steal children? I don't kill other people? Any of those should do."*

*"Mr Parker, please. You must focus. If you are to save your daughter you must think as they do. These men see themselves as businessmen although they are selling human life and innocence. The main thing you have on your side is that you are a white foreigner, a gora. That is the one trump card you can play." He leaned forward, dropping his voice. "Here is the plan, you will go to one of the brothels run by Das' gangs. When there you will make a show of being the* big man *and say you have a business proposal for him. You will suggest the idea that you are able to be a scout for him amongst the tourists. The white face is friendly to whites. You propose you can earn their trust and bring them to him as their first port of call for drugs and women. Sex tourists from the West are a huge business here and they pay five, ten, twenty times the prices which can be put on Indian Nationals*

*who know how things work and how to haggle. You get him that direct line to the goras and soon you will be his golden boy. He will be eating out of the palm of your hand and you will have the means to find your daughter."*

*"There's no other way? I have to actually get involved in this filth? How will I be able to live with myself?"*

*Dipal shrugged his shoulders diplomatically and looked at the ground drawing a circle in the dust with his foot. "How will you be able to live with yourself if you don't?" he asked quietly.*

*I looked at the temple and saw a small group of children playing outside, running and laughing. I hung my head, my shoulders dropped.*

*"I am truly sorry that I can see no other way. If there was, I would do it." He said, placing a comforting hand on my shoulder. "Don't try and contact me. In a few days I will have a new passport sent to your apartment and an address for the brothel for you to visit where you will be able to establish contact with Das. Before then, try and change your appearance as much as possible. Lose the long hair, shave, get shades; anything you can do to appear different. There are so many people they coerce that they forget many faces, but here yours is unique, so be drastic. Any ounce of recognition could leave you dead. Get your back story together; know who you are and how you are useful to Das.*

*Always be ready with an answer and brim with confidence, any sign of fear and they will rip you apart. One last thing," he said, pulling the cap back onto his head. I looked up into his compassionate eyes, "good luck. May God be kind to you, Mr Parker." With that he stood, nodded courteously and in a moment had disappeared into the bustling crowd.*

*I stood and began to trudge through the throng of people wondering what lay in store for Aisha and me in the future. Suddenly my arm was grabbed again and I looked down into that toothless face.*

*"Death surrounds you. It is too late."*

## Chapter Eleven

Roy watched me as I stared at the photos contemplating their significance.

"So, you are beginning to see what type of man really is your husband," Roy said, eagerly scanning my face for a reaction. "This is why you must be helping us Mrs Parker and telling us every little bit you know about anything and anyone who your husband was speaking to. Anyone else at all who knew he was here or what he may have done. I must be getting to all of these people and," he smacked his lips against his teeth, "be speaking with them. Most earnestly," he said through tight lips.

I turned my face up from the dust to look at him though it strained my neck. "I still don't believe Tom could have done those terrible things, despite what you say. Listen, Superintendent, if this is all true and Tom was a killer in some gang, I would have no hesitation in helping you and giving you the name of every single person in there, but as I have said I have no idea about any of this so that means that I can't tell you anything. Please, just let me go," I said, my head slumping back down into the dust, my temples throbbing and the pain in my shoulder continuing to flare up every time I made the slightest movement. Roy reached over me to collect the horrendous photos, the acrid smell of his sweat almost choking me as my nose was inches from his arm pit. As he stood the revolver wobbled in its holster, settling so that it was pointed directly at my chest. .

"Letting you go? That is a very interesting suggestion Mrs Parker but not one which I think I will be doing at just this moment. You see, Mrs Parker, I will not stop until I know what I need to and if you are unwilling to help me then I think that we can have you put into the very nice prisons over here for a very long time till you are very old and all forgotten about. They are very nice. Only twenty womens to a cell and sometimes you are even able to get a bed without these little lices on them. If you are very lucky you may even get fed, but that depends how much you can fight the other womens in the cell. Yes, I think you will be enjoying a stay there. In fact, if I take you now it may loosen your tongue into the talking, yes?" he said, removing the key from his pocket and squatting down in front of me.

"You can't do that. I'm innocent, I haven't done anything! You can't just lock people up because you feel like it. I know my rights. Just you wait till the British Embassy hear about this! Then it will be you in prison!" I screamed, hysterically pulling the handcuffs against the back of the chair in a vain attempt to burst free. Roy threw his head back, laughing spitefully.

"These are big claims which you are making Mrs Parker! I

assume then that the British Embassy know you are here? That they are waiting outside to come in and rescue you?" I clenched my jaw and broke eye contact, quickly trying to think of a solution, of someone who knew where I was, but it was futile.

Roy pretended to yawn. "There is often so much paper work in these prisons that it's not always worth doing it. It could take years to get through it all, if we do it at all. It is a luxury to know who is in the prisons, so sometimes," he waved his hand nonchalantly, "they just go in and leave when they have to be carried out."

"People will be looking for me," I spat out, trying to portray a confidence to mask my rising fear. "You can't just make people disappear."

"But Mrs Parker, that is exactly what we are doing to these filthy criminals. You British are too soft on crimes and look at what situation you are finding yourselves in. Tut, tut. If you are sparing the rod you are making bad the child," he scolded.

"But I'm not a criminal! I have done nothing wrong!" I shouted.

"Oh, but Mrs Parker, please do not be fooling yourself. At the moment you are obscuring the course of justice and making lies about your associate. Maybe we could say that you were even committing the crimes with him? Who knows. Also, there is assault on a Police Officer which the police are looking very strongly upon."

"What assault on a Police Officer? When exactly was that meant to have happened?" I asked in disbelief.

"But Mrs Parker, you do not remember? You tried to attack me. That is the reason for which I am locking you to this chair. Why else would I be taking such strong measures? If you were behaving nicely this would not be being necessary."

"This is completely insane! None of this makes sense. How exactly am I supposed to have committed these crimes here in India when this is the first time that I have been here?" He paused for a moment, rubbing his fingers against his moustache.

"That is a good question, but I know that the truth will come out somehow and we will find out all of your dirty little secrets and how you have committed many crimes. There are many cases which I am trying to solve and it would save me a lot of time if you were able to confess to those. A few more stamps in your passport and you could have been involved in any number of these crimes. It is a simple thing really."

"You won't get away with this, you crazy bastard," I spat out, trying to hold back the tears that were stinging my eyes.

"Oh, but I think you will be finding that is exactly what I will be doing. Or is it the case that you told all your friends where you were going and when you would be home? I guess they will be worrying when your flight from Kolkata does not have you on it and they are there waiting to be welcoming you back home, isn't it? They will be most worried. But wait, is it being the case that as soon as I called you packed up your things and were on the next flight without telling anyone? Hoping it was all a mistake and that you could get it all made new again without worrying anyone." He pushed his face close to mine, his eyes red and bulging, sweat coursing down his forehead. "I see that I am right. There will be no one knowing where you are. But no, wait," he said, dramatically throwing his hands in the air, "your husband must be frantically looking for you. He will alert the British Embassy and they will find you. Is that how it will happen?" he said, his yellowed teeth grinning inches from my face. I twisted my neck and spat into his waxy face with as much venom as I could muster from my lying position on the floor. After a shocked moment he slapped me hard across the cheek, then wiped the saliva with the back of his dusty sleeve.

"Mūrkha kutiyā!" he cursed before slapping me again, then grabbed my chin so I was forced to look up at his furious face. He pointed vehemently to the table which Tom's body was laid out on. "On that table is an evil man about who I need to know many things."

"He was my husband and I loved him," were the only words I was able to hoarsely whisper.

Roy softened his tone, sighed, and sat cross legged in front of me in a weak attempt to show solidarity. "I am sure you did, Mrs Parker, but he was also a killer. I have shown you the photos of his tattoo, I have told you what he has done, but there is still much worse that I must tell you. I hoped that I could have gotten answers before having to tell you this but your husband was also involved in selling children into very bad places to be making money for himself and the gang of a powerful man called Saiful Das."

"In the same way I attacked a Police Officer? Why should I believe your bull?" I asked, anger and confusion at what to believe rising up in me. I hoped more than anything that Roy would be exposed as a liar and I would be free to reconsider all he had told me about Tom in light of the lies which dripped so easily from his venomous tongue. He sighed, ran his fingers through his greasy hair then stood and strode to the corner of the tiny room. Picking up a leather satchel he flipped it open, pulling out a neat brown envelope. Reaching inside he carefully pulled out a number of photographs and walked back towards me with the envelope tucked under his arm. He stood for a moment and sighed deeply.

"Mrs Parker, I am sorry for the threats I was making to you. It was wrong and my lies were just to scare you because I need so much to know more so that I can stop these horrible crimes happening. I am believing you that you do not know anything but really need you very much to help. Please, take this as a sign of my good intentions." He knelt behind me and undid the handcuffs from the chair, then gently helped me to sit up. I breathed deeply, my head spinning slightly from the sudden movement and also the blinding pain.

"Is better yes?" he asked.

"Yes, thank you," I said as I rubbed my bruised wrists, trying to massage out the lines where the cuffs had pinched my skin. I noticed that luckily there was no bleeding as the colour returned to my hands. I shuffled backwards, every muscle in my body screaming as I tried to stretch. Extremely wary of this new side to Roy I decided to press home the advantage while he was playing good cop.

"Please may I get some water?" I asked as sweetly as possible through my parched lips.

"But yes, of course. What kind of host am I being neglecting these needs? Is there anything else you would be liking for your comfort?" He asked, his voice too sickly sweet, like a parent trying to placate a stroppy child.

"No, thanks. Water is fine," I responded. He turned and headed back to his satchel to fetch his canteen of water. As soon as his back was to me I tried to bend forward, but another bolt of pain shot through me like an electric jolt. I cursed under my breath, then managed to reach forward with my leg and knock the broken chair leg back towards me so that it was within easy reaching distance of my right arm. I positioned it behind me and shuffled back even more so my back was to the wall with the broken chair leg hidden behind it. I wasn't exactly sure what I would be able to do with it in my physical state but just having it there gave me a small safety blanket to calm my nerves. Roy's schizophrenic change in demeanor still did not have me convinced, but I was eager to exploit any opportunity to break free from whatever this situation was.

However, even stronger than the desire to escape was the need to see what evidence Roy had to show me about Tom. I had to know who my husband had been. What he had been capable of.

Roy returned with the canteen and held it for me to take. I grabbed it with my shaky hands. The water was still ice cold and poured mostly down my chin as I greedily drank as much as I could, like a thirsty deer at a river. The cold splashes on my chin and chest felt a welcome refreshment from the intense heat. I shivered slightly from the chilling sensation as it streamed down my throat and into my stomach. As I was drinking I kept my back pushed firmly against the wall to conceal the chair leg, but was sure that Roy's eyes lingered behind me for a second too long as he squatted next to me.

Eventually he pulled the canteen away and gave me a crooked smile. "All better, yes?"

"Great, thanks," I croaked, my cheeks beginning to redden as I tried to assess if he had figured out that I now had the chair leg. Having seen his erratic mood swings I was unsure what would happen if he caught me with it and did not want to risk finding out.

"What was it you were going to show me?" I quickly blurted out, to break his attention.

"Ah yes," he said, removing the pictures from the envelope, his face darkening as he did so. "I sorry that you are having to see now what sort of man it was that you were having for a husband. A very bad man. What I have here I hope will be showing you this beyond any doubt."

## Chapter Twelve

*All I could do was sit and wait, trusting in Dipal and his insane plan.*

*I waited at home for the next two days, not even leaving to collect food in case I missed contact from him. I used my razor to remove every single strand of hair from my head. I grew my stubble. I wore shades in the house. I practiced accents. I stood for hours in front of the small cracked mirror in my bathroom trying to persuade myself that I was credible as a member of the criminal underworld. I considered cutting my face to look more sinister. I paced around, fretted, exercised and prayed. I almost went insane sitting staring at the wall and practicing what I would say in a million and one scenarios which I dreamt up.*

*After an impotent eternity came a hurried knock on my door. When I answered the corridor was deserted but a small brown envelope sat on my doorstep. Glancing around, I snatched it up and tore it open. Inside it sat a number of things. A wad of thousand rupee notes, Gandhi's face seeming to look at me with disapproval. A new passport, which when opened up had my old passport photo with the name Richard Lawson scrolled beneath it, the name of the lecturer who had taught Dipal English. Also in there was a note crafted in Dipal's impeccable scroll-*

*I have word Das will be at one of his brothels tonight. It is known as Alankara Kotha and is on 212 Park Street. Do not arrive before 11pm. Use this money to dress well. Have courage and remember why you are valuable to him. He will collect you as a magpie collects those things which sparkle.*

*This passport will offer some protection if you are revealed. It is a genuine fake and will be enough to get you back home if necessary. Do not try and contact me. I will be in touch when possible. Have courage my friend that you will find your daughter and retrieve your soul. May God be kind to you. We shall meet again.*

*Attached to the note with a paperclip was a photo of a number of men. The man in the centre had a red circle drawn around his bulbous head in red marker pen. On the back of the photo was a single word.* Das.

*I studied the photo, anger rising in me at the face of the enemy which had now been revealed. His grotesque grin revealed golden teeth, a mouth of metal paid for by the slavery of children. His obesity symbolized his greed and all that he had taken from others. The devil now had a name and a face and I was due to meet him in a matter of hours.*

*I held the photo between my thumb and forefinger and sparked the lighter which was lying on my kitchen table, watching with pleasure as the flames licked and danced around Das' body till he was utterly consumed, leaving only a dark ash. "I'm coming for you," I said into the flames, "and by the end you will wish that your death was this quick."*

*Hours later my bravado had deserted me as I stood outside the belly of the beast. As I rehearsed my lines I caught a glimpse of my reflection in the window of a car; the shaven head, tailored suit and shades made me feel like a child playing dress up. I was a fraud and it felt like every inch of the expensive suit screamed out that I was an imposter. This was madness. I may not have been literally committing suicide, but it was the same as charging unarmed at fifty men with rifles screaming, shoot me!*

*I looked at the entrance to the kotha, or brothel, deciding that I would head home and think of another plan when a black Audi rolled past me, pulling up at the entrance. A scrawny driver dived out of the car, pulling wide the back door with a semi bow. A heavy leg swung round, followed by a second, threatening to destroy anything foolish enough to get in its way. Two plump feet squeezed into impeccably clean white brogues strained to take the weight as the gigantic frame of Das struggled to stand. The driver reached out an arm to give support and was angrily swatted away like a fly. A moment later Das hauled himself to his feet, and brushed down his black pin stripe suit, the buttons all bulging. He marched towards the brothel, a number of the girls on the balconies pulling their saris over their blouses and disappearing back into their rooms.*

*As he marched towards the door the Madame of the brothel walked briskly towards him, arms spread wide. They embraced then chatted jovially for a few minutes before she gestured to the multi-story brothel, a sea of eyes gazing out nervously from windows and balconies. Das followed, patting her boldly on the buttocks, a smile on his face as he gazed up at the building. The chauffeur waited nervously by the car, snatching glances at the windows and fidgeting with his shirt collar as he chewed paan, occasionally spitting it's red mess on the pavement.*

*Das was greeted with nods by the two muscular men standing mindfully by the doors, though I was unsure if their purpose was to prevent rowdy customers getting in or the girls from escaping. He patted both on the arm then disappeared inside, fading into neon lighting. I breathed deeply knowing that this was the one chance which fate had dealt me, and even if it was not a great hand this was the only time to play it.*

*I sauntered over to the door, hands in pocket, shades covering my eyes as I tried to look as natural as possible. The two bouncers who were idly chatting suddenly stood to attention, obviously unaccustomed to goras frequenting their brothel. Arms folded and eyes filled with suspicion one muttered to the other in Hindi. All I managed to catch was something about charity workers. Before being addressed I shook my head, announced 'girls' in Hindi, flicking them a devious smile and placed fifty rupees in to each of the gents hands, with this seeming to be the magic password, confirming you can buy your way into almost anything in India. They stepped aside; their eyes still following me as I entered some kind of lobby area, my heart breaking with every step I took. It was a hive of activity, numerous girls wandering back and forth, off of corridors and into rooms. Two women, probably both in their late twenties stood in a corner sharing a joke and cackling wildly, their teeth as red as their bright lipstick. A small girl of about twelve walked past me, her face so made up with bright eye shadow that it was almost like that of a clown. She pulled her sari tightly around her chest and scuttled into one of the rooms. A small child of no more than eight wandered around carrying towels and sheets on her head as her naked feet padded the floor.*

*The air was heavy and dense and reeked of a mix of perfumes, smoke and sex. The sound of laughter, grunts and screams made the very walls appear to be alive. Numerous men appeared and disappeared, their eyes reflecting everything from perverse desire to deep shame. I stood nervously tugging at my collar, glad that my eyes were covered so as not to fully betray my fear and anxiety. A soft hand slipped on to my arm and I looked into the face of a girl who can have been no more than sixteen. She had large doe like eyes and her hair was brushed back with a white flower sticking out from behind her ear. She was heavily adorned with gold bangles which chimed every time her slim arms moved.*

*"You want girls?" she said smiling, pulling me towards the cash register booth. "Many girls. Indian, Nepali, Bangladeshi," she gestured to the girls milling around in the corridors. "Make good time fun," she said, stepping closer and thrusting her small breasts against my arm. I involuntarily stepped back, nervously shaking my head. Her face contorted in confusion and rejection.*

*"No girls," I stated, "I need to speak to Saiful Das." She looked me up and down apprehensively then turned on her heel and sped off down the corridor, returning moments later with the Madame.*

*"You want to see Das?" she asked, her voice harsh and grating. She folded her arms and studied me. "What business does gora have with Mr Dasji? You Police? NGO?" she asked, wagging a painted nail at me.*

*I shook my head, thrown by her aggression. I recognized the suffix of Ji as term of respect and knew I must speak appropriately here.*

*"I have a business proposition for Dasji. I have a way to*

bring in many more customers to your..." I said, floundering for a word to describe where we were, throwing my arms around to indicate what I meant.

"More business? More moneys? You have friends looking for good times?" she asked, arms now on her hips as she changed her stance to thrust her chest out and offer me a seductive smile.

I nodded, trying to look as business like as possible. Her smile widened as she glanced down taking in the well-tailored look of my suit.

"Then you are being most welcome here," she said. "Dasji is having fun with the girls right now. He likes to take his time and takes three or four in his room. He will not want to be disturbed, even for good business." She clapped her hands and the girl I had seen earlier appeared at her side, her chiming alerting me to her presence. "We have a special treat for you," continued the Madame. "Puja, take him to Rupa in room five. She is our diamond. Then you can tell all your friends our girls are first class, young and fresh. She only thirteen years. Young virgin. Full fun times. Never been with a man before. Most girls only fifty rupees but this one is special. Five hundred because she is new. Her first night working, just in from Bangladesh," she said holding out her hand for the cash. Puja took my arm and winked at me.

"No, I can't I..." I began stammering.

*"But Dasji will be long time. No time to talk business now. You enjoy our girls. You want more than one? You don't like Bangladeshi's?" She asked, appearing offended at my refusal.*

*I knew for my cover story to work I would have to go along with this, despite the disgust growing in my stomach. I shook my head.*

*"That's fine," I said, counting out five hundred rupees from the wad in my jacket pocket, making sure it was seen. It had the desired effect and the Madame's grin expanded as she gladly took the money and the extra hundred rupees I added to the tally, knowing this generosity would be reported to Das and would hopefully secure me an audience with him. I allowed myself to be escorted to the room at the far end of the corridor, many curious faces watching as I passed and a few of the women blowing kisses and clawing at me, hoping to attract my attention and custom. Puja chastised them all, slapping any encroaching hands and saying the name of Rupa. At the name the women tutted, jealousy showing in their eyes.*

*As we reached the door she pushed it open, gently calling Rupa's name. Rupa stepped forward, her arms covered in twice as much jewellery as Puja. She wore an ornate sari which was gold and red and in pristine condition, her hair neatly parted and silky. She looked down at the ground, too nervous to raise her eyes. Her face was heavily painted, like that of a china doll. She stood in stark contrast to the women in worn and dirty saris with red paan stained teeth and bawdy jokes. Were they a vision of what she was soon to become? A pain stabbed at my heart as I imagined another brothel, maybe even another room here with Aisha dressed like this, forced into these acts.*

*Puja patted me on the arm and smiled as I passed her fifty rupees, closing the door behind me as I stepped in. When the door closed the sound of a sitar began from an old tape player in the corner. Rupa timidly began to move her hands in a traditional dance and slowly began to move her hips, the whole time staring at the ground. It was tragic seeing a child sadly playing at being part of a messed up adult life.*

*As she began to spin around, she twisted her wrists so that the bracelets chinked in time to the music. She slowly raised her trembling head and looked at me, anxiety in her eyes, then fear as she saw tears streaming down my face. She stopped dancing and looked at me uncertainly as I began to weep, overwhelmed by the innocence lost by such a cruel trade. Confused, she began to slowly unwrap her sari. I rushed over and held her child like hands, shaking my head. She looked bemused, unsure what I wanted from her as I sobbed.*

*I tried to explain in English, but it became clear that she did not understand a word. I tried in Hindi too but again she just looked at me blankly, with fear in her eyes. I walked over and stopped the music, wiping the tears from my eyes. I wondered if there was any way that I would be able to free this child, but knew that even if it was possible that any chance of meeting with Das and getting Aisha back would be destroyed.*

*I attempted to soothe my conscience by rationalizing that if I could get close enough to Das this whole empire would come crumbling down and eventually Rupa too would be free again, but that did not make looking in her terrified face any easier. She walked over, her body quivering and coarsely grabbed at my shirt attempting to undo the buttons. I gently took her tiny hands in mine again and shook my head, placing her arms against her side. I held a finger to my lips for silence and took out a thousand rupees and placed them into her hand. She looked around the empty room by force of habit, then scampered with the money and placed it under her mattress, revealing a comb that was placed there and also a photo of who I assume were her parents.*

*This gave me an idea and I searched inside my wallet for the photo of Aisha I still had placed there. I pulled it out and showed it to Rupa, pointing to ask if she was here in the brothel. She took the photo and stared at it for a few moments before slowly shaking her head, perhaps wondering if I was trying to find and capture her.*

*We lapsed into silence for a few moments as I waited until a reasonable amount of time had passed, frustrated at not being able to communicate and fearful that my strange behaviour may be reported back to the Madame. I reasoned that I could justify my lack of performance to impotence and that the money was a way to cover my shame if ever revealed, but luckily no further questions were ever asked on that evening's events, only if this was the best brothel I had ever been to by the Madame which I assured her it was.*

*These questions and a few others were asked by the Madame as I returned to the lobby, feigning my satisfaction at the services provided. Luckily her more probing questions were halted after a few moments as the door opposite us was slammed and Das emerged adjusting his belt and breathing heavily, his hair plastered to his wide forehead with sweat.*

*My stomach tightened and I had to strongly fight the urge to pummel my fists into his grotesque face. Somehow though I managed to plaster a self-assured smile on my face as the Madame played host and introduced us, "Dasji, this man is here to offer first class business opportunity to you. Bring in many rich goras. Pay top dollar," she said, smiling at me like we were old friends. Das did not seem to warm as easily. He stepped forward, towering over me, the smell of alcohol and smoke on his breath as he clamped a meaty hand on my neck. Without saying a word he slapped my chest, legs and small of my back with his free hand, looking for a weapon without loosening his grip at all. Task accomplished he slowly released me then put his face within an inch of mine.*

*"Gora arrives here from nowhere asking to talk big business. How can I be to trust you? I not even be knowing you," he said, eyes bloodshot with dilated pupils.*

*"You don't know me," I said back, "but I think you may have been introduced to my friends before," I said, reaching to my pocket and pulling out a bundle of cash, "and if you want to see more of them I suggest you learn some manners. If not I will just go talk to my dear friend Chotu Pandey and see if he is more interested in my business proposal," I said, dusting myself down and pushing past him. I had bluffed and waited to see if it would be called or not. My heart was racing as his hand grabbed my shoulder.*

*"Let's not be too quick thinking," he said, nodding to the Madame who pulled back an orange sari on the wall, revealing a dark room concealed from the rest of the kotha. She ushered us inside then let the sari fall, leaving Das and me alone in the shadows.*

*He went to a wooden chest and poured two generous glasses of whisky, putting one before me then taking a hearty swig from his before sitting down. He spread his hands in a gesture for me to speak. I carefully weighed my words to make maximum impact knowing this would be my only chance to get close to him .*

*"Every year thousands of goras come to this country. Business trips. Holidays. Travelling. All of them after a bit of fun and excitement. But how many do you see walking through those doors?" I asked pointing to the entrance, "a few, sure, but not many. Why not? Because they need a guide. Someone who looks the same as them, talks their language. A person who can show them the best parts of town without them having to worry. That's where I come in," I said, slurping back on the whisky. "I can be your man on the street, the one who brings these goras here to spend their wads of cash. You and I know that one white punter pays ten times the price of the clients here at the moment," I said, finishing the whisky off and trying not to wince as it burned my throat. "For my tiny cut in this I can have this place overflowing with them and your pocket full of dollars. It's a win, win situation."*

*He looked at me curiously, his head moving from side to side in contemplation. After a moment he placed his huge hands on the table and leaned forward so that I could see his narrowed eyes in the dingy light.*

*"This sounds like the good business. But first you need to be proving to me that you can be doing what you say."*

*"Just tell me what you need me to do." I leaned back and spread my arms wide, trying to keep the panic from my face.*

*"If you have so many gora friends it should be easy. I will be giving you one hour. You only need to bring one gora back*

*here to prove you can be doing what you are saying. If you do we talk more business. If you don't..." he paused, leaning even closer so that I could see the beads of sweat on his forehead, "...I never want to be seeing your face here again."*

*I opened my mouth to protest and ask for more time but he waved my pleas away, the chunky gold chain on his wrist jingling. "You have one hour," he said leaning back and filling his glass again.*

*I left the kotha in a state of disarray, knowing that I had to find someone otherwise my search for my beautiful daughter would be over before it even began. I was aware that at some stage I would have to bring people here but had not anticipated it happening so soon. I needed Dipal and his wisdom but had no way of contacting him.*

*I usually went weeks without seeing another white face on the streets, so finding one in the next hour who actually wanted to go to a brothel was quite a long shot. I leaned on a wall around the corner from the brothel, head in hands trying to think where I could find other goras.*

*My mind wandered back to my meeting with Dipal in Kalighat. The whole area had been full of Westerners. That had to be the place to start. It was only ten minutes by metro. I sprinted up the road to the station, praying the trains were still running regularly at this time of night.*

*As I stumbled down the last step into the empty station a*

*train lurched to a halt in front of me. I looked up at the display board and saw this was on the same line as Kalighat, so I leapt on. Collapsing in the empty seat, I struggled for breath while undoing my top button, my new suit soaked with sweat. Pushing all moral problems with what I was doing aside I quickly tried to formulate a plan of action, knowing time was against me. I couldn't just run around the street asking if anyone wanted to go to a brothel so decided that one of the seedy bars would be my best bet. If I could find someone drunk enough, then maybe it would work.*

*On arrival I charged out at the station eagerly looking for the dim signs for a bar. Though the visit with Dipal had been my only one to the area I knew there were numerous drinking holes nearby. Within a few minutes I spotted a sign for Kingfisher beer with a small, worn sign pointing to the basement below, proclaiming it was a bar. The entrance was dim, and the inside dull and smokey, a few rickety wooden tables and chairs scattered around. The actual bar was the main focus, bottles of Glenffidich and Jack Daniels proudly on display. In one corner sat a group of three lads drinking and laughing loudly, the accents sounding German. A few other Indian men sat solemnly by themselves, cradling the whisky filled glasses in their hands and in the far corner sat a large white guy with greasy long hair. He was hunched over and seemed to be sobbing silently as he slugged back from his glass.*

*I looked at my watch and saw I only had thirty eight minutes left. This was probably the only chance I had. The lads looked like they were just getting started for the night so I ordered two large glasses of whisky at the bar and plonked one in front the lone man. I introduced myself and sat down, asking what was wrong. Probably due to the speed with which he was knocking the drink back he immediately told me about how he had received an email earlier in the day from his long term girlfriend wanting to split up with him, leaving him heartbroken. Seizing the opportunity I plied him with more drink and filled his head with how he was much better without her and about the fun he could have as a single man.*

*Within fifteen minutes he swore that I was the best friend he ever had and we stumbled from the bar, arms around each others shoulders. I ushered him towards the Metro, promising to take him somewhere to help him forget all about her and stuffing thousand rupee notes in his pocket so he appeared affluent to Das.*

*With two minutes to go we tottered into the brothel, my arm still around him for support in his disheveled state. Sobering up slightly he began to ask questions, not so sure it was a good idea and explaining how he just wanted to go and call his ex-girlfriend, but I kept talking, convincing him that this was a great idea and that no-one would ever have to know anyway.*

*As we passed the doormen we were warmly greeted by the Madame in the lobby, a throng of women behind her. She whisked him away as he looked over his shoulder at me, slightly bemused. I smiled at him and gave him a thumbs up sign but inwardly felt sick at myself for preying on him and also exposing the girls to more of what I wanted to protect my daughter from. I had no time to dwell on my guilt though as the firm hand of Das clamped down on my shoulder. I looked up into his grinning face, saliva crusted at both sides of his mouth.*

*"Very good work. You are not just all talking. I see this being a very profitable for us both," he said, extending his brawny arm. I took his hand and shook firmly, knowing I had made a deal with the devil. My soul was now lost.*

## Chapter Thirteen

There were five pictures in total and he began to lay them out in front of me like a set of playing cards, each one delivering a fresh blow to the case I was trying to accumulate in my mind to prove Tom's innocence.

The first showed a picture of a Tom in his mid-twenties. It was strange to see as I had never seen any photos apart from those which I took of him. He had no photos from earlier years which he claimed was due to a house fire in which they were all lost, leaving him like a man with no past.

I was intrigued to see this earlier version of him, one which I had never known. It gave me a snippet of his life before me; a life I now wish had remained hidden. His head was shaved, his body far slimmer and his skin appeared smoother, less cracked and marred. But it was his eyes that stood out. Even though he was years younger in the photo his eyes looked so old, harrowing and hate filled.

The picture appeared to have been taken on a zoom lens and was a close up of this younger version of Tom shaking hands with an Indian man who I would place in his early forties. The man could only be described as huge, his large fingers coiled around Tom's hand like sweaty sausages, each finger adorned with a gold ring. He wore a large grin, but without humour, his jowls drooping at the sides like a bulldog. His teeth were bared, with gold sparkling from his molars. The skin under his eyes was blackened, like an overripe fruit. His hair had been slicked back and shimmered from the grease. He was dressed in a black pin stripe suit with a white tie which cascaded down the bulges of his stomach, a pair of shades peeking from his top pocket.

"Who is this man?" I asked, being able to guess the answer before it was revealed.

"This was a photo taken in the surveillance of your husband Mrs. Parker, about seven years ago. We as the police are making this photo to use as evidence against him and to see what he is doing. You are telling me that your husband has never mentioned this man to you before?" he asked, tapping the belly of the man next to Tom with his yellowed finger nail. I shook my head. Roy sucked on his teeth and tutted before dabbing his face once more with his faded handkerchief.

"This man is big criminal here in Kolkata and in all India, yes. He is Mr. Saiful Das and is the head of big gang for selling drugs and womens. Very powerful and rich man. He and your husband were very close. Your husband work for him as right hand man, buying and selling like it is a game. Both men are becoming very rich. Very powerful too. Super players in the gang world."

"But Tom wouldn't have done that. This doesn't make

sense. Why would he just decide to join some kind of sick gang like that?" I gazed intently at the photo trying to see some clue that would explain it all but no solutions appeared.

"Money and power I am afraid Mrs Parker. These are the two most important things in life to men. They are what is making the world go round. Your husband as a white man was able to be bringing more gora customers to Das and his brothels so they made a deal bringing them both more money and power. It was quite simple." He said in a matter of fact way, as if explaining that two plus two equals four.

"Let me get my head around this. Basically, what you are saying is that my husband was a dealer and a pimp?" I asked skeptically, trying to match up that information with the life which we had together.

"That is exactly what he was Mrs. Parker. They were both known by the police but it became impossible to get the evidence on them. We had photos, but what we needed was someone who would be giving a testimony against them but no one would be having courage like that. Here, look," he said, turning over the other pictures to expose more of Tom's crimes.

The next picture was once more of the younger version of Tom, again in a shot with the beastly Saiful Das. In the picture Tom was standing outside a narrow alleyway in which there were a number of heavily made up women standing around chatting. Nearby sat a number of teenage boys smoking cigarettes. In the middle of the picture was Das with a protective arm over the shoulder of a silver haired European looking gentleman, ushering him through the saris hanging out to dry and into the dark alleyway.

"Brothel," was the one word Roy spoke as he flicked over the next picture. In it Tom was speaking to a number of white men in suits at the airport, all of a varying age. Roy held the photo up to me and asked if I recognized anyone in the picture. I looked closely but shook my head.

"Look again, please Mrs. Parker. I need to know that your husband did not ever introduce you to these men or that they were not working with him." I looked again, carefully scanning each face but had no recollection of any of the men. He nodded his head slowly, then thoughtfully turned over the next photo. This one was a picture of Tom driving a heavy duty truck with a slight man of around forty sitting next to him.

"This was your husband bringing in a shipment of womens from another part of the country to work in brothels here in Kolkata. Police are not stopping white face because they usually doing good works for the charity people, unlike your husband. But Mrs. Parker, have you ever seen this man next to him? He is called Goshan. Has your husband ever mentioned him?" Again I shook my head having never seen the man. He nodded curtly. Then he revealed the final photograph, this one a Polaroid picture. I picked it up and gazed at what it revealed. Tom was dressed exactly as he was when he set off for his business trip a few days ago, though it now felt like months. In it Tom was standing over Das pointing the gun at his head. His arm was stretched out fully, pressing firmly into Das' meaty forehead, Tom's eyes ablaze with rage. Behind Tom was a girl of around eleven, looking wide eyed at him, her beautiful emerald eyes filled with horror. I gasped at what I was being shown, shocked at the only possible conclusion the photo led me to.

"Did Tom kill Das?" I whispered almost breathlessly, closing my eyes in a vain attempt to prevent it from being true.

"Yes," he answered without hesitation. The picture slipped from my fingers. Although I knew it was coming the answer still felt like a hammer blow. Already feeling almost delirious with the heat and emotions of the day I tried to use the last bit of my rationality to figure out how my husband could have gone from lying next to me a few nights ago to murdering the head of the Indian Mafia.

"Did he, I mean, did Tom see how wrong it all was? Was it some sort of attempt at stopping what was happening?" I fumbled, hoping that in some way it may have been a messed up way of achieving redemption. Roy's answer was curt and left no room for ambivalence.

"He killed Das so that he could take all the money that he was making. Once Das was dead he took it all for himself."

Every answer from Roy felt like a sharp blow to my stomach leaving me fighting for breath and having to re-orientate myself. I leaned back on the wall for support, my energy completely drained. I pulled my legs in to my chest and let my head roll back on to the brick wall. It was all true. My shining knight had actually been a monster the whole time. I felt physically sick as I remembered the times he had touched me, whispered in my ear that he loved me, the times that we had made love.

What did it say about me? How could I have been in love with a murderer? A person who took children from their homes and sold them into prostitution, this was the man I had chosen to love, to marry. Bitter tears coursed down my cheeks as I hugged my knees into my chest and wept for forgiveness from whoever could absolve me of this feeling.

"Come now, Mrs. Parker. I am knowing that these are very difficult times for you today but we are only having little time to discuss issues so if you are ready to continue then we must be pressing on," Roy urged, a note of frustration in his voice.

I breathed deeply and managed to settle my nerves before looking Roy in the eye. "Just tell me what I need to do and it will be done."

## Chapter Fourteen

*And so it began. The first steps of my journey ever deeper into the black heart of the Indian underworld. Within hours of our agreement and several whisky's later, Das drove me across town to a tattoo parlour which he regularly frequented. I was informed that entry to the gang came at a price as he pulled up his top to reveal a tattoo of an eagle clutching a snake in its claw.*

*"This shows our strength. We will be destroying anything that gets in our way," he said proudly as he clenched his massive fist. "This tattoo will show that you run with us. People will not mess with you if they know you are part of my gang," he said, pulling a revolver from under his kurta. "This will get you respect," he said, looking at me seriously, "and free drinks and girls all over town!" he laughed, displaying his golden teeth.*

*I was glad by this stage to be so inebriated that I was unable to properly feel the needle as the artist commenced his work. Had I been sober my mind would have paid far more attention to the look of this dingy room, the lack of sanitation and the fact that I would forever be branded with this grotesque logo which symbolised the thing which I hated most. Luckily I was on the verge of passing out as he began and had lost all consciousness by the time he finished.*

*The next thing I remember was awaking to the sound of children running and screaming. I blearily opened my eyes, dazed and confused as three small girls peeked around the door frame, giggling and pointing at me. I leapt up, covering my naked body with a sheet, blinked and tried to figure out where I was. My clothes were neatly folded in a pile and were placed on the floor with candles scattered around them. There was red lingerie balled up in the corner and the room smelled strongly of perfume. I could hear women shouting and laughing and also a baby screaming.*

*I was back in the brothel.*

*I quickly scrambled around on the floor, gathering up my clothes and holding them to my chest. My head was pounding as I put my fists to my eyes, trying to remember last night and praying that nothing had happened when I arrived back here. My stomach lurched at the possibilities and I felt sick at what I may have been capable of. I remembered meeting Das, talking business and then waking up here. Was it just the whisky? Had I been drugged? My head felt like a scraped out coconut, making it impossible to follow a single train of thought.*

*The children still stood giggling at the door, goras obviously a novelty for them. I waved them away with my hand, but they remained, sensing any lack of conviction in my ability to chase them off. I tried to pull my shirt over my head* to cover myself and suddenly felt a tight and itchy sensation on my left shoulder blade. I reached around to touch it and felt padding which seemed to be crusted with blood. I drew my hand back in shock trying desperately to recall a memory of what had happened the previous night. At that moment the Madame walked in, a smirk on her face as she viewed my reaction. "You are now a brother of Das," she said pointing to my back. "That shows you are one of them. Part of the gang, you are in and there is no coming out. Welcome," she said, grinning, her words sounding like a warning rather than a greeting.

Suddenly the visit to the tattoo parlour came back into blinding focus. I put my hand over my face and slumped down on the bed. There was no longer any escape, I was officially part of the gang. "What happened last night?" I asked groggily not really wanting to know the answer. A playful smile lighted on her face.

"You here, you drink a lot with Dasji, talk business, drink a lot more, go out, get the mark of the gang then you got dropped here for a good time with the girls again by Dasji."

My heart dropped as I awaited to hear of my debauchery.

"I send two girls to your room. They come in, take your clothes off and then you fall asleep, so I am sorry but nothing happens. If you want we can arrange for something, something for you now?" she asked.

*I shook my head and held my stomach as a gesture of the effects of the alcohol.*

*She shrugged and turned her back. "Dasji say he meet you here tonight. He want to see more customers."*

*I groaned inwardly, knowing I had got lucky last night but had no idea as to how I was going to go about it now. All I wanted was to get my daughter and get out of here as soon as possible, hopefully with a soul not completely tainted by my deeds on the way. "Wait," I called the Madame. She turned and looked at me inquisitively.*

*"How many girls do you have here?"*

*"Thirty two," she said proudly. "Best girls in whole of India. All clean too," she added.*

*I grimaced at the next few questions I was about to ask. "What is the age of the youngest girl you have here?"*

*Her thin eyebrows creased as she carried out some mental arithmetic. "We have Rupa who is thirteen who you already know well," she said, smiling crookedly, "but, we have two who are twelve and almost ready to bloom. If you pay first class rate I am able to save their blooming for you especially?"*

*I shook my head, wondering how to phrase my next question. "I noticed yesterday that there was a number of smaller girls, maybe five, six, seven, who were working here, carrying towels and things," I began.*

Her face suddenly became serious and she raised her hand. *"Those girls too young for sexing. Not till older. Unless you pay very, very big rate says Dasji."*

I shook my head frantically to calm her, *"no, not for that. I just wondered if you have many that age who work here?"*

*"Ah. Maybe twenty who are before the eleven age. They carry things, make beds, take money, show people to rooms. Not difficult work. Is good for them to learn and see what they will do when older."*

I wondered how far I could go without appearing to pry and causing suspicion. *"These young girls, where do they come from?"*

*"Many are the daughters of the Dalit workers here, they can grow up and learn from their mothers, lots of aunties here to teach them too. One or two are sold here by their parents to raise money for the family."*

*"Are any taken?"*

*"Taken? What means this?"*

*"Taken from their family to come and work here?"*

Her face grew dark and I knew that I had offended her.

*"You think I am stealing children?"* she folded her arms and looked at me sternly.

*"Everyone here has choice to leave exactly when they want. They all have choices to stay or go. No taken."*

I held up my hands to try and appease her and apologised.

*I knew that I had to keep her on my side to have any chance of completing my mission and I was very wary that my questions would lead to suspicion so I tried to change tack and sound like the punters she would deal with every day.*

*"Do you have any girls with caramel skin? Big emerald eyes? That's what I would love, the younger the better," I said, inwardly repulsed at my words. She laughed. "That's what every man in here is after, the whiter the skin, the younger the girl, the bigger the price."*

*"Do you have any girls like that? Big green emerald eyes?" I asked, desperation getting hold of me.*

*"We have one, her name Moonshine. Lovely skin, almost white like you. She the most wanted girl we have. Young too. Only eighteen."*

*I shook my head. "Too old, you have any others like this?" She shook her head. "These girls are like rare flowers. You only find a few in the whole forest of these dark girls. We did have one though, very young, a few days ago, brought here just for the night. Beautiful little girl, eyes which sparkled like these emeralds you mention. But Dasji just brought her for storage before he moved her on. Who knows where she went, could be one of the other brothels here, it could be in Mumbai" she shrugged her shoulders. "I asked to keep her for future, big money with her but he just laughed and said he had other plans. She would have been the jewel of the kotha in a few years. If you want caramel girl so much I am sure Das has others here in Kolkata but I tell you again we have the finest girls here and all clean. Some other kothas have all sorts of girls, dirty ones giving you pains in the private parts."*

*"How many other brothels does Das own in Kolkata?" She seemed irritated by any questions not relating to her brothel and tutted in frustration. "Maybe fifteen, but I warn you, some others bad. Not so nice as here. Them girls not know how to please a man like here."*

*Fifteen! I had no idea how to get round so many brothels to see if Aisha was still in the city. I thanked the Madame and passed her the rest of the money Dipal had given me for any information she received on anyone who looked like Aisha, promising far more if she could deliver her to me. The wad of rupees eased the creases on her forehead and she wobbled her head, once again eager to please. I had one final question which I hesitated before asking, not really wanting to know the answer.*

*"How many brothels does Das supply girls to in India?" She laughed.*

*"How many stars are there in the sky? There are too many to count. He has many in Mumbai, Delhi, Jaipur, all over. Even he does not know the exact count. He even sends some girls overseas to Bangladesh, Europe. Many men like you all looking for good time with these girls." I felt repulsed at being*

labelled with the type of men who would visit these brothels but also a slight bristle of pride that my disguise had been convincing this far.

"What decides which girl goes where?" I asked, desperately trying to form some kind of plan to find Aisha. I felt like I was dipping a stick in the ocean and expecting the rarest fish to come leaping into my arms.

"All I know is that the very best girls come here and the rest can go where they please. Now, I no paid for talking and have many girls to be seeing to. Save your questions for Dasji. You come back here tonight with many friends and I will see what I can do about finding you caramel girl," she said winking.

I trudged home, head throbbing, back itching, heart sinking. More than the stars! Where did I start? I at least had entry to the gang and the Madame unknowingly on the lookout for Aisha but what was that compared to the thousands of places that she could have been taken to?

I reached the door, my head spinning and noticed it was already open. I pushed it extremely cautiously to find Dipal sitting at my table, wearing sunglasses and a cap which covered most of his face.

"We have little time," he said gravely, "tell me all." I told him all of the previous night's events, confessing how I had *brought a customer to the brothel and how hopeless I now felt about the mission. He nodded silently as I spoke. "It may not feel like it, but this is good news. You now have his trust and a doorway to the underworld. We do not know how long it will take, but you must keep faith. Never let hope be destroyed. Das is always on the move, keeping an eye on his brothels, making sure everything is running well and doing good business. Keep close to him and I have no doubt he will soon be sending you all over to drum up more business in Mumbai, Delhi and wherever else there is an untapped gora market. When you are there you can ask about girls with emerald eyes until you find your Aisha. Flaunt the cash, offer big bucks for girls with green eyes. That is the unique feature which does not make our search hopeless. One day we will find her," he said, as much in reassurance of himself as me.*

*"But every day that passes before we find her, she could be..." I let the sentence tail off and shuddered. Dipal placed an arm on my shoulder and shook his head. "You cannot be thinking that way. Let us do what we can. You must first think of how to get customers to satisfy Das. Last night you were very lucky in finding that man." I grimaced at what I had done. He scribbled an address on a sheet of paper, "this is where you are likely to find a number of less, shall we say,* moral *goras. Head there tonight and get as many as you can for the brothel. I will make sure you are not troubled by*

police. *You must become my eyes and ears in that place. Find out how Das works, who else is in command, what do they do, anywhere children are forced to work illegally and then report it back to me. With enough evidence we can build to a series of raids culminating in the arrest of Das and all those worms that work for him and destroy them ending their evil work. You are the key to that," he said, patting me on the shoulder. He handed another envelope of cash to me. "Take this. You must be seen as prosperous." He stood to leave.*

*"I cannot thank you enough," I said, "you have done so much," I said. He bowed his head.*

*"It is my penance. I will never be able to do enough," he said cryptically, with the meaning of this not becoming apparent to me until much later. With that he rose, slid his cap further over his eyes and was gone.*

*I arrived that evening around 11pm with a gaggle of eight wide eyed men who repulsed me, all following my lead as if I were the pied piper, mesmerising them with my tales of the beautiful women in the brothel. I wished that I could take each one of them straight over a cliff like the rats they were, but instead had to laugh along at their coarse jokes and listen with humour to the tales they told of their previous visits to the brothels of Amsterdam and Thailand. As goras, understandable fears of the Police, corruption and Indian jails had cooled their passions of visiting the array of women Kolkata had to offer, but under my reassurances they soon warmed to the idea.*

*Tucked discretely away as a private brothel it was difficult to find compared to the large multi-storey brothels of Sonagachi, the red light district in the North of the city. I had been informed by Dipal there were over 10,000 sex workers in that small area. I had visited briefly on my searches for Aisha but was overwhelmed by what was like a zoo of prostitutes all milling around the streets and pacing behind their barred windows. My tour party said that they had visited the area once, but were greeted by police loitering in the streets, no doubt taking their cut from each visitor to the area.*

*As terrible as it sounds I was glad that Das was so organised and had no brothels in this area due to the huge competition driving his prices down. This way at least I knew Aisha was not amongst the throng of sex workers there, which would have made the impossible task of finding her even more difficult.*

*This brothel drew little attention to its self from the outside, meaning there was no police presence and due to the higher prices it tended to attract a higher class of clientele if there was such a thing in the world of perverts. As I led the way, the group following excitedly behind me, I felt almost like a school teacher taking their class on a trip of debauchery. I sighed, thinking about how rapidly my life had changed from reading bed time stories to get Aisha to sleep to taking a group of men to have someone to sleep with.*

*As we arrived the Madame was waiting, our approach drawing some attention with such a large number of goras in the area. I could see her counting as we approached and obviously conducting the financial value of such a group. She hurriedly beckoned the girl from the desk the other day and whispered instructions to her, to which she rushed off, preparing the way for our arrival.*

*The Madame greeted me like a Prince, her eyes sparkling as the others stood grouped behind me looking around nervously. She beckoned us all in and had a number of girls standing in various states of undress, smiling coyly. It was almost like a cattle market where you were able to choose which meat you desired. The Madame stated the prices and the men pointed out which girl they wanted, not even bothering to barter the prices set as their eyes danced with lust, all paying extra to stay the full night. They eagerly handed over their cash, then were led away by the girls of various shapes, sizes and ages. I noticed the caramel skinned girl which the Madame had offered me, as beautiful as many of the Bollywood actresses proudly displayed on posters over the city. There were a number of girls in their early twenties, all slim and of a darker complexion. A few girls I could* recognise as Nepali, one or two girls in their late teens and then walking slowly at the back of the group was a younger girl, head down, saree wrapped tightly around her. Rupa. My heart caught in my throat as I looked at her, wishing there was a way of protecting her and keeping her innocence, but I knew it was useless. One of the men patted me on the arm, "young and fresh," he exclaimed, winking at me, then turned and took her by the arm.

"And for you?" the Madame asked seductively, her lips next to my ear.

"Working," I said shaking my head. "Is Das around?" She wobbled her head as an affirmative, then led me through to the same room from the other night, Das sitting there smoking a cigar. Before addressing me he looked straight at the Madame. "Well?" he asked impatiently. She waited a moment then smiled, placing the cash she had just collected on the table, fanning it out to reveal the full extent of the money taken. I stood nodding my head. Das leapt to his feet and slapped me on the back heartily. "These white boy goras have made me happy man!" he exclaimed. He reached down to the table and threw a small pile of notes to the Madame. After a moment of raised voices another small pile was handed to her before he divided the mass in front of him between us, the notes looking tiny in his huge hands.

"This is how you be keeping me happy!" he exclaimed,

smiling broadly, "Make sure you keep doing it," he declared as the smile vanished from his face, his cheeks drooping.

"You want to have fun time with some girls now? Celebrate new business?" The Madame asked us both.

"Now we have important work to be making. Later..." he said, slapping her backside as she giggled, "is for playing. Come," he commanded me. "Now I take you and show the rest of my empire in Kolkata. Soon you will be bringing your friends to all these different places. And we..." he said, putting his arm around my shoulders, making the fresh tatoo burn as he pulled me in to his enormous body "...we will be rich!"

And so we set off on our tour of the red lights of Kolkata visiting all fifteen of the brothels which Das either owned or delivered girls to. As we travelled, Das and driver sat in the front, myself and two men who could only be known as Das' bulldogs sat mutely in the back, the silence punctuated every now and again by an exclamation from Das about one or other of the brothels and the quality of the girls he had working there. Despite the fact that they both looked straight ahead, I could feel the hostility emanating from both sides of me, a severe dislike as I had managed to leap frog into the position of Das' blue eyed boy. As long as I could remain useful to Das I realised no-one else could touch me.

*The visits all seemed to follow one of two eventualities. Eventuality one: We would arrive. Das would no sooner have ejected his cane from the car than someone from the brothel was upon us, showering praise on Das and handing him a large sum of cash. Das would smile, inform him of a new delivery of girls in the next week and we would leave.*

*Eventuality two: We would arrive. Das would have to leave the car and walk towards the door, something he was not eager to do. A small sum of cash would be handed over with much begging. The two bulldogs would leave the car. A larger sum would be handed over. Someone would be beaten. An even larger sum would be handed over. Das would smile. We would leave. Whatever the outcome, Das got paid.*

*I had hoped that on the tour I would get the chance to visit each brothel and scout around inside for any signs of Aisha, but the opportunity never arose. However, I knew that with the new tattoo and the recognition as one of Das' men that I could enter all of the brothels, click my fingers and find out if anyone like Aisha had been seen there. However, at such a young age I reasoned she would be hidden away out of the public's sight until she became regarded as ready by Das or the Madame or whoever that decision was left to.*

*I mentally noted down the addresses and promised I would manage to visit each one within the next few days, but it ended up as another one of my promises made in vain as Das* had other plans for me.

Part of those plans involved heading back to Alankara Kotha for a meeting with a few of the closer associates. I eagerly waited for the opportunity to see the faces in the den of evil as I plotted to bring an end to their wicked ways. I knew this would give me the opportunity to further know how the operation was run and what could be done to provide the evidence that would bring them to justice.

The meeting was again in the hidden room, the Madame pulling back the curtain to reveal six men sitting in a cloud of cigar smoke drinking whiskey and chatting loudly. All were well dressed and this could almost have fooled anyone as a civilised business meeting if the products sold were not drugs and young girls.

On our arrival all chatter stopped and everyone stood in respect of the entrance of Das, one or two even bowing heads. Sharp eyes then turned to address me, suspicion written over every face as Das gestured for me to take a seat at the far end of the table leaving a solitary empty chair next to him at the head of the meeting. A hushed whisper in Hindi rose around the room before Das pointed in my direction.

"Gentlemen, we are having a new business partner. He is now providing good business by bringing goras to the kotha's. He and his white money are most welcome here," he said to *an obligatory laugh and to settle any dispute to my presence. "Now, fill your glasses, we are having much business to discuss. First of all, Lalji, I believe that you have sent men to Uttar Pradesh to collect some womens for us there?"A balding man with scratched spectacles inclined his head as confirmation.*

*"They will be delivered here, then we will divide them amongst the kothas in Kolkata making sure no sisters are being kept together. Can we be expecting them here by Tuesday?" Again Lal's head was inclined and Das nodded, ready to move on to other business.*

*I was sitting here in the midst of these men, somehow having won the trust of Das and hearing every single plan which they were confiding knowing this would be like gold dust when I was able to report it back to Dipal. It felt like things were almost being made too easy as I tried to remember facts and figures of people being trafficked and wondering how many I would be able to report to Dipal for the police to act on. I suppressed a sly smile.*

*"Goshanji, what news is being of your brother and his kotha in Mumbai? Business is good? Will he be needing more women's soon? "Das said, folding his hands and leaning forward, his chair creaking as he did so.*

*Suddenly the curtain was pulled back again and a slim figure slipped through. A short man with a neatly combed hair and an even neater moustache. He dragged his cigarette then threw the butt on the floor, stomping on the embers with his foot. He nodded to the head of the table. "Dasji."*

*I sat, stunned, hoping that I was somehow wrong about the identity of the new arrival. Das removed any uncertainty in a single word.*

*"Roy," he said, pulling the chair out next to him and motioning for him to sit.*

## Chapter Fifteen

Roy glanced at his watch then back at me. "There are a number of things which you will need to be doing to help. The first thing is to look through these different passport copies of your husband and be telling me if you recognise any of the different names which he is using." I nodded, my temper flaring within me at Tom. In the whole time which we had been together we had never been outside of Britain on a holiday. Every time that I had broached the subject there was always a reason that it was not possible. He had lost his old passport when he moved. He didn't have time to send for one or have the documents needed. It was cheaper to just stay at home. A whole list of feeble excuses while the whole time he had numerous passports he was able to use at will for his misadventures.

Roy handed me three photocopies and a brand new British passport.

Immediately I opened the passport and flicked through it. It was completely empty apart from a six month tourist visa for India and an arrival stamp dated three days ago. It showed that it had only been acquired five days ago and contained a picture of Tom wearing his navy blue sweater with his hair at his shoulders. The name written there was Daniel Evans. Daniel Evans? I mulled the name over in my head then told

Roy I didn't know anyone of that name. It felt extremely bizarre to see pictures of the man I had loved with a new name, created for the purpose of deceit. He had deceived me convincingly enough.

The second was a photocopy of another picture of Tom, this one showing that it had been validated eight years ago. Tom had a shaved head and charcoal black rings under his eyes, with thick stubble. The image was quite disturbing. Even more disturbing though was the name Tom Parker. If he had been using aliases, why was Tom Parker the name on his fake passport? I quickly leafed through the remaining two copies, the first validated from nine years ago with Richard Lawson as the name and the last one showed a picture of Tom in which he looked about eighteen, wild hair flung around and a bright orange scarf draped around his neck. He had a self-satisfied smile and looked so unblemished and *new*. The date for this one was when Tom was eighteen and had the name John Steven Parker written on it. This appeared to be the original.

I felt numb. His name had not even been Tom.

## Chapter Sixteen

*The room fell silent as Roy sat down, a number of the men around the table shuffling uncomfortably in their chairs, eyes downcast. He seemed to relish the discomfort as he slowly and deliberately removed another cigarette from the packet, lit it, inhaled, then blew the smoke as a challenge into the middle of the table as an assertion of his status in the group. His eyes roamed unhurriedly round the table as everybody sat waiting for him to state the purpose of his visit. They moved steadily until they settled on me at the far end, partly obscured by his smoke.*

*For a moment his eyes faltered as they focused on me, surprise flickering as he turned his full attention in my direction. With my back to the wall and eight hardened criminals between myself and the makeshift door I knew that if Roy were to recognise me and blow the whistle my time would be up. There would be no time for excuses or polite explanations or an escape by promising to keep my mouth shut. These guys did not give second chances and I would be lucky to leave inside a bin bag in only one piece.*

*It had only been a number of days since I had been questioned by him and I had little doubt he would have forgotten my face in that time, even with the shades, shaved head and suit. I shrank back in my chair trying to avoid his* gaze, my heart pounding as I waited for my identity to be unveiled. Would Das kill me himself? It would almost be poetic, taking my daughter then my life. At least then he could take no more from me.

I seemed to be under Roy's inscrutable gaze for what seemed an eternity. His cold eyes held me as he leaned back and whispered in the ear of Das. Das shook his head then whispered back, Roy nodding slowly, a sly smile playing on his face. He reached into his jacket pocket and I closed my eyes, preparing for the bullet, praying for it to be painless. But it never came. I opened them, seeing Roy unfolding a sheet of paper and laying it on the table, the attention of every eye upon him.

Business appeared to have resumed as I sat, waves of relief flowing over me, but I still could not believe that Roy had forgotten me that easily. My heart began to quiet, but was still frantic every time Roy or Das glanced in my direction.

What was he doing here? I wondered for an ignorant moment if I had been too quick to judge and he was actually also undercover, but all such ideas were soon exposed as folly when he opened his mouth.

"In my hand I am holding a warrant obtained by the Kolkata police to be searching a number of the brothels to which you gentlemen contribute. Part of the Government trying to show their commitment to creating a more moral *society. They are looking for the womens under eighteen and will be targeting these individual ones," he said, pointing them out on the parchment as the men strained to read the names. "The raid will be taking place on Wednesday, so be sure to be having them clean, otherwise even I won't be able to be turning a blind eye and not seeing." He looked around the table awaiting nods from all gathered before continuing. "Also, we seized twenty kilos of cocaine from Chotu Pandney," he said, pulling out a number of white packages from his bag to an excited murmur, "so here is the four kilos I could be getting without people asking me any questions. I have also managed to be organising a number of raids on his kothas. I will guarantee safe passage for your trucks with the girls from Mumbai on Thursday as long as you will only be using these roads," he said, handing a sheet of paper to Das and standing to leave.*

*Das handed him a brown envelope. He pulled out the bank notes, held them to his nose and then fanned them before nodding and placing the envelope in his bag.*

*"Next time I need to be collecting more monies. An extra five percent. That Dalit dog Dipal is checking on everything so things are getting more difficult," he said as he looked pointedly at me before turning to leave before any further comment was made.*

*An angry mutter rumbled around the table before Das*

*called the meeting back to order, continuing to explain the details of what was to occur over the following week. I knew that I should be taking detailed mental notes but was unable to focus, still unsure if Roy had recognised me and if he was likely to be waiting in my apartment when I arrived home. My mind began to wander as I considered if Roy was involved at this level, what percentage of officers were also part of it. Were any of the other guys around the table also part of the Police? How were these crimes to be stopped if they were aided by the very people who were meant to stop it?*

*At the end of the meeting I stood and hurriedly tried to leave, fearing what Roy had whispered about me into the ear of Das. As I approached the exit though the full bulk of Das covered my escape as the other men filed out, shaking the hand of Das and each leaving generous sums of money I later learned were a gift to Roy for his information and the immunity he provided against the Police whilst diverting his attention into other gangs.*

*We were left in the now empty room and I stood, wondering if he had been waiting for this quiet moment to kill me. Automatically my eyes scanned the room for a means of escape but found none. Das motioned for me to sit and I followed orders. "Roy and I have spoken," he began, lifting his kurta top and withdrawing a revolver, aimed in my direction, "and we are in agreement of what to do with you." I considered going for him but knew he would pull the trigger before I was able to leave my seat. I stared at the revolver contemplating how something so small could take a life.*

*Suddenly, Das spun the revolver around so that the handle faced me. He held it out and I slowly took it in quivering hands. "You must go with Goshan to Mumbai. Business there is not so good. We need you to bring more goras to our kothas there. You will leave tomorrow night, take a few girls from here, then bring a few more back here on Thursday. You cannot leave a whore in one place too long. She makes ideas, thinks of escaping back to her family if she is too close to home. This way, down in Mumbai, we are her only family. Also, I am not trusting Goshan so much. He usually travels with other men and I suspect that he is not bringing me back the money I am due. Other men have loyalties to him, but you are new blood and I know I can trust you," he said, more as a challenge than a statement. Had Roy said something? "This way you are being my eyes and ears. If you even see him dip his filthy hands into my money," he formed his fingers into the shape of a gun and pretended to shoot. "He has become less useful to me recently anyway and is now more of a leech than an asset," he said wistfully. "You will be arriving back here Thursday then we can be putting you back to work at bringing the white dollar to our beautiful brothels," he said, grinning to reveal his golden teeth. "For your troubles you will be* given first time with any virgins you bring back from Mumbai, if there are any virgins in Mumbai," he said cackling. I gave a half-hearted smile. I saw this as an opportunity to press Das for any information on Aisha.

"What I want is a virgin with big green emerald eyes and caramel skin. That's my type, the younger the better," I said, feeling revulsion that these were the words many people uttered for real. Das stopped and appeared to look at me with new eyes, seeing an area of weakness to exploit, knowing he now had me on the line and he would be able to reel me in to do his bidding.

"You are looking for a young Aishwarya Rai!" he said, talking of one of the most famous Bollywood actresses whose poster adorned every shop and wall in India. "These types are like rare jewels, very expensive. The younger, the finer the diamond, so making bigger the price. To have this type of girl as a virgin, unspoilt will be a lot of money. Even as a partner in the business I cannot be giving this free. If I am to find a girl like this for you then you must be paying me back for my kindness. There will be certain, ah, favours which you will need to be carrying out for me."

I knew with this request I was putting myself entirely in his debt, wondering how big these favours were that he would call in. I nodded in submission and he smiled grotesquely.

"Very good," he said. "There have only been a few like

*this, especially the virgins, not many at all. I am dealing with thousands of whores every year, but some, ah, make a super impression for their beauty," he said, looking past me, as if trying to recount their names. "If I am correct we have a few young girls down in Mumbai with these emerald eyes you seek. Virgins or not they are well worth a try."*

*"How old?" I asked, causing Das to laugh at my eagerness.*

*"Young. Maybe fourteen, fifteen, but old enough to know enough tricks to show you a good time," he cajoled. I shook my head.*

*"Younger." I responded. He raised his eyebrows.*

*"Younger than that, they do not know how to be pleasing a man."*

*"I'll decide that," I countered. He raised his eyebrows further, a wicked grin on his fat face.*

*"I can see we will get on well!" he chuckled. "It is a shame you were not being around a week or so ago. My boys found me the most beautiful jewel. She was very young," he motioned to about his waist, "emerald eyes that dazzled, caramel skin," he sighed, "but she is not ready yet. She must be trained, broken down, her spirit is still too strong. From a gora, thinks she is a Princess!"*

*My heart almost leapt through my chest with every word which fell from his mouth.*

*"Where is she now?" I said, with far too much emotion, exposing my desperation. It took everything I had not to turn the gun which Das had just given me back on its giver. It was Aisha, it had to be! I tried to remain calm to not blow my position, but it was futile, Das smelled my vulnerability like a shark smells blood.*

*"This little jewel is still here in India but I sent her away from Kolkata. Too dangerous as she may draw attention to herself." He looked me up and down. "You want her? You can buy her virginity when she is ready."*

*"How about I just buy her now, straight out? Cash in hand? How much do you want?" I said. He shook his head slowly.*

*"No amount of money you give me will be worth what she will make for me over many years. This is good business. When she is older and put to work every night, men will be queuing around the block for her, drawn as you are now! Over a life time she is worth more than any pittance you can be offering me now. But, if you remain loyal to me, do all that I ask you, when she is of age you will have the privilege of first night with her. Until then go and enjoy Mumbai and all the womens we have on offer there. There are many there to be enjoying."*

*"Where is she?" I practically growled at him.*

*"She is in training. Collecting money from men like you,*

*washing clothes, changing sheets for whores; seeing the life she is to live. You will see her when the timing is ready. Before then, you have work to do. Remember, eyes on Goshan. Bring me back my money and I will be seeing you on Thursday," he said raising his hand to thwart any further conversation. As he waddled through the door I let my hand rest on the butt of the revolver, then let it go limp. With Das gone I would just face a jail sentence and the small glimmer of hope that had presented itself now would be snuffed out. I had to have patience. Even if it killed me.*

*The next evening I met Goshan at the appointed time and we set off in the truck. I was oblivious to the fact that inside were around ten girls between fourteen and eighteen, sitting silently with arms folded in the back of the vehicle until we stopped five hours into the journey for Goshan to find a bush. On the way back he opened the hatch and shouted into the darkness in Hindi. A moment later, a small girl came out, almost like a mole escaping the ground, blinking furiously but not making a single sound. She began to walk around the bush for modesty and Goshan shouted again, causing her to come back round and squat a metre in front of him as she carried out her business. He barked at her a moment later and she scurried back into the darkness of the truck, arm shielding her face for protection. The silence and Goshan's lack of communication other than scowls led me to a state of blissful ignorance in assuming that we had not taken any girls as the plan suggested. Now, the souls of ten more angelic girls rested on my conscience as I drove them to a brothel without even the decency of a meal or the dignity to go to the toilet alone. I closed my eyes and prayed that somehow I would receive forgiveness for these unspeakable crimes and that someday they would also be released when I could bring Das and his empire to rubble.*

*I had alerted Dipal about the trip and informed him of our day of arrival back to Mumbai for which he had told me he would be nearby with a camera to catch us unloading the girls from the truck and also passing them in to the custody of Das, providing the first of many nails into his coffin. I was very glad to be able to hammer them in.*

*First though I left the hub of the truck and walked round to the back, motioning for Goshan to open it. He cursed at me in Hindi, then pulled it open, exposing the girls, all huddled together in the dark, each wearing a sari at the most in the cool conditions of the truck. They all blinked, and almost in unison raised arms to protect themselves. I gasped, then, on regaining control, motioned for Goshan to bring the bottle of water we had in the front of the truck. He cursed again, but knew that Das had sent me with his authority, so he consented, bringing the bottle back and muttering under his breath. I held it to one of the girls and she stared at me with frightened eyes, pushing back into the safety of the group. I crouched down and unscrewed the lid, passing it towards her, motioning for her to drink by taking a sip myself. Tentatively she reached out a bony arm and took it, taking a sip, her eyes always fearfully on mine, as were all the others.*

*It was like being in an animal enclosure at the zoo, trying to communicate with creatures which have only ever been hit or abused by humans. The bottle was passed around and every girl had a sip as I nodded trying to comfort them as Goshan paced grumpily back and forth outside the truck. Once finished they passed the bottle back and I took it, wishing I could do more to respect their humanity.*

*Goshan ripped the bottle from my hands then threw it into the bushes. "Dalits," he spat as means of explanation. "Unclean. Not for sharing," and stalked angrily to the front of the vehicle. Incensed, I followed, but remained quiet, knowing my authority from Das only travelled so far.*

*After we arrived, the girls were taken to the brothel of Goshan's brother, who quickly hurried the girls inside, raising his hand and striking one who struggled to get to her feet after being cramped in the back of the truck for thirty hours. They were all led away into the dingy quarter, a Madame hitting the back of their legs with sticks as they ran past her and into the corridor.*

*Goshan's brother stood and counted out a large number of*

*thousand rupees notes, each note handed over seeming to cause him actual bodily harm. Goshan looked at it smugly, flicked through the wad and creamed a few of the notes off of the top, placing them in his trouser pocket.*

*That night I was given an orientation of the city and set out to find more goras to attract to the brothel, knowing that all of my efforts would be reported back to Das by Goshan, as he tried to discredit me and gain favour again. However, it was easy going and I managed to bring another ten or so punters in, my conscience still pricked but I was getting accustomed to this. The other few nights passed in a similar fashion, each night easier than the last to shrug off the guilt which plagued me. My conscience was becoming numb as I tried to see it as only a sales pitch, giving people what they would pay for elsewhere. Without spending much time in the brothel I was able to distance myself from all that was occurring.*

*The night we left though reminded me of the reality of the lives which were touched by what I was part of. We left Mumbai with the empty truck, the aim being to fill it at the numerous villages at which we stopped on the long road back to Kolkata. In each village we visited there were agents waiting with women, Goshan paying varying rates depending on the age and beauty of the ladies, trading them like cattle before loading them on to the filthy truck.*

*The first place we stopped at was a small village to the north west of Delhi. As we arrived there were three girls standing waiting, looking around nervously. As I got out of the truck the girls actually smiled and whispered frantically amongst themselves. Confused, I asked Goshan what they could possibly be pleased about. He smiled grimly at me. "They offered good job, working for rich goras, teaching in schools. Lots of money to send back to families. Families happy. They happy." They were ushered into the back of the truck, waving shyly at me. I look ashamedly at the ground, knowing that their faith in me was leading them to a living nightmare, not the dream worlds which they had probably concocted in their heads with the promptings of this silver tongued agent. A fairytale land where the streets were paved with gold and all their problems were gone.*

*My heart broke every time we made a stop, the different girls deceived through a range of stories and coercions. Some were taken with the promise of a good job, others very lives were payments for debts accrued by their families to Das, others still had been promised a marriage when they arrived to a suitor who was supposedly to meet them in Kolkata. Goshan relayed each story to me with relish as the number of girls in the truck grew.*

*A number of whimpers and cries escaped as several of the girls began to realise that they had been deceived. Belt in hand, Goshan disappeared to the back of the truck and then there was silence for the remainder of the journey. I could not bear to watch it but did not have the bravery to intervene, so I sat motionless, pretending to sleep through some of the most awful moments, the scared faces of the girls burned onto my eyelids. Those same pleading eyes still plague me now and continue to haunt my dreams, thinking about the lives I was part of destroying and praying that you may somehow forgive me for that, even if I cannot forgive myself.*

*I also took another life that day. With the power of my words I also killed Goshan, though his death seemed insignificant after the pain I had seen inflicted on the girls. After arrival back in Kolkata, Das congratulated us on the haul of girls we had got, then took me aside, asking about Goshan and if he had taken money from him. Though I could plead innocent, I knew that my nod of confirmation was sentencing him to death as Das took three steps in his direction, raised the gun and without a word pulled the trigger, letting Goshan's body crumple to the ground. The girls screamed at the sound while Das' two Rottweiler's emotionlessly stepped forward to dispose of the body as if disposing of rubbish. I am ashamed to say that I actually smiled. Shocked as I was, I couldn't help but be slightly grateful to Das for his actions, performing the deed that my* cowardice held me back from, all be it for very different motives.

I had never seen anyone die before and especially not murdered before my eyes, but the sight of the blood, the finality of it, seemed to release some kind of frenzied energy in me. Right there and then I wanted to line up everyone involved in this sick business and execute them all in the same way, letting their blood drain from them as they had drained the hopes and dreams of these girls. As they planned to do with Aisha. Was it wrong to feel that way? I fondled the handle of the revolver and felt a strange surge of power knowing that once Aisha was safely back to me I would hunt down everyone I could and have my vengeance.

The girls were led away by the Madame as she soothed them, ushering them into the brothel as if she were a caring big sister. I knew that once inside they would begin the process of breaking down the girls to make them ready to entertain men, up to as many as ten a day Goshan had informed me, his eyes mad with lust. I vowed in my heart to reunite these girls with their families as soon as the time was right, but eight years later that day has still not arrived. I sometimes wonder what became of them as they were led away into the darkness and if any of them have ever emerged from it.

After that night things began to settle into a bit of a

*routine. I would pound the streets at night bringing in business and forging relationships with any goras who could be potential clients. Most were tourists, so the work was constant. Many of the men I met enjoyed telling a good story and spoke of their exploits elsewhere. As they came and went regularly I was able to tip off Dipal to any particularly dubious suspects, he would catch a picture of them entering and leaving the brothel and they would be arrested before they reached the plane. Dipal worked fast so word of their arrests never made its way to other goras and more importantly, Das was none the wiser.*

*This was the pill for my conscience which helped me sleep at night. That and the opportunity to tip off Dipal about a number of deliveries of both girls and drugs around Kolkata. However, Das was a smart man so these had to be very limited. Occasionally Das began to suspect someone was advising the police, for which we had a plan. When people were in for questioning Dipal would pretend to let slip the source of the information, implementing someone who would have known the plan. Das would arrange for them to be disposed of, the world would be free of one more trafficker and I would climb the ladder further into Das' trust. I had been taught by the traffickers that others' lives could be expendable and they were paying the price for giving me my enlightenment.*

*As a gora, I became a mascot to Das, a good luck charm, something which none of the other brothels had to bring in customers, meaning that the business was doing a roaring trade. I knew this meant the girls would have even more men forced upon them but justified it to myself that it would soon end and they would be freed, my judgement impaired by sheer desperation.*

*Das would often talk business with me, asking advice and explaining how he ran the whole organisation. Names of the other big clients were mentioned and stories of what they had done were told. Dipal was informed of everything and often able to catch pictures of deals which had been set up. Slowly we chipped away at the workings of the organisation waiting for the landslide.*

*As gifts for my work and to keep me in his pocket Das lavished me with liquor and girls, those with as light a skin as possible thinking this was what pleased me. I had to live the charade as best I could, pretending to be satisfied with the girls, but in private telling them I was impotent and unable to perform, paying them lavishly to keep this quiet although I knew it would spread like wild fire in the brothel. I was known as, 'the toothless white tiger' and due to this reputation many of the girls would be eager to entertain me, knowing I would not force myself upon them as the others did. If Das knew he certainly did not mention it and it seemed that this secret* worked as a perfect cover to avoid arousing suspicion to my lack of desire.

If new girls had arrived in the brothels of Kolkata and I was alone with them I would show a picture of Aisha trying to discover if they had contact with her. Many times they spoke no English or Hindi, but the conversations were always the same even if they did. A sad shake of the head, a no or nahiin; it did not matter. However I was told, the outcome was always the same. I was left empty.

Every step closer to Das and every piece of evidence against his gang still seemed to be a step away from Aisha. As time drew on I wondered if Das had any knowledge of her or where she now was despite his promise. Even if his word was true I may have had to wait another eight years before she was given to me if it was not just another girl with green eyes and light skin. As the evidence and files piled up against Das I knew Dipal was itching to move before anything changed. The longer he waited for a big crack down, the more likelihood there was of me being exposed or indeed of Roy discovering more on the cases of the goras imprisoned.

Even after several months, I was still unsure of Roy's position. I was always treated icily by him, but did not know if it was because I was white, jealousy of my closeness to Das or if he had correct suspicions over my intentions. I ignored him as best I could, but it became increasingly difficult as we *worked more and more closely together.*

*Since I had informed Dipal of Roy's role within the trafficking racquet his outrage had manifested itself in giving Roy the worst possible cases and berating him publicly on numerous occasions. Roy would often speak of the increasing scrutiny he was under, often citing Dipal as the cause of it, referring to him as 'the Slumdog' and berating the Mandal Commission for giving jobs to filth when those from higher castes were left without work. A bunch of inbreeds not fit to clean his toilet, yet here one was giving him orders, he often lamented.*

*During one of the weekly meetings, after one particularly vicious verbal attack about Dipal he continued to speak about the poverty in which he had grown up and how he should have stayed there. "This useless mutt, he grew up in the slums behind my house and now he thinks he is too good for all of us in the Police force because he was handed out a job because of the Mandal Commission! When he was growing up he was too poor to go to school. The youngest in a family cursed before him with two girls. His father an alcoholic, mother dead, all three begging on the streets his Father had the idea to sell his two sisters to a brothel in Delhi, no more dowry worries and enough cash to put the boy through school! If I was being him I would have sold all of them off, starting with Dipal! He comes from there yet has the nerve to* be telling me how to do my job," he continued to rant as I sat, slowly realising the picture in my wallet was actually the sister of Dipal. This work was his penance.

I did not mention what I now knew to Dipal for fear of bringing shame to him, but continued to work diligently, handing over all the information I could until one night the routine I had found myself in was abruptly stopped. As a reward for my hard work, Das had treated me to another evening with one of the girls in Alankara Kotha. However, I was awoken early, the door flung open hurriedly by the Madame. I lay, covered on the floor by my jumper, the girl curled up like a small kitten on my bed. The Madame hissed at the girl and ordered her to leave immediately, with which she sprang off the bed and darted out of the door. Next to me on the floor was the picture of Aisha which I had shown to the girl the previous evening. Blearly eyed, I wondered at this early intrusion which was prohibited in the brothel. The Madame reached down, grabbed the photo of Aisha and held it inches from her face studying it.

"Up," she barked at me. Immediately I jumped to my feet, clothes already on from the previous night. She stood, arms folded and stared at me intently. "The toothless white tiger," she stated, having heard the name from one of the girls. "You are no businessman. You are no friend of Dasji. I see you. The girls have spoken and I know that you are a liar." She poked *me in the chest, "I know exactly what you are."*

## Chapter Seventeen

I did not know who he was. His name had not even been Tom.

For some reason this betrayal seemed the deepest. I had been married to this man for three years and had not even known his real name. I did not know my husband's name. I snorted at the absurdity of it and looked at Roy shaking my head. "I have no idea who any of them are or even which one is his real name. Seems like you knew more about him than me."

"So you know nothing about the other names mentioned on here? These are not names of friends or accomplices or people with whom he would be working?" He questioned, taking back the photocopies. I shook my head again, seething at the betrayal.

"Mrs Parker, as you can see, your husband was a very," he paused searching for the right word, "elusive man who was most good at fooling people about who he was. As I have told you, he was very involved with these gangs and no doubt raised a lot of money. With using all these different names I think he may have been keeping the moneys in different accounts," he drew out Tom's bank card. "It would be most useful if you could be telling me the pin number for this card Mrs Parker so that I am able to, ah, investigate and be discovering any transfers which he has made so that we can trace them and use them in evidence to break up this terrible gang."

"5398," I readily complied.

"Excellent. And is there a joint account which you are using together?" he asked, jotting the number down in his yellowed pad.

"Yes, but I check the transfers on that and there has been nothing unaccounted for. I don't think that is necessary," I replied, reluctant to allow my bank card out of sight with Roy.

"But I am afraid it is very necessary. I assume you have not checked the transfers in the last few days?" I silently shook my head. "Well, it is being very likely he may have transferred the moneys across just before he was becoming dead. I will check for you now so that no one is able to accuse you of keeping moneys involved with these gangs. This is all for your safety too Mrs Parker. Accusations in India are very dangerous things and I want to keep you free from them."

"2813," I sighed as I handed the card to Roy, too exhausted to argue. "Can you check the transfers by just having the pin number?" I asked suspiciously.

"Yes, yes. All with the Police technology. Very clever Officers here in India," he said, patting the cards which he had placed in his shirt pocket. I was still dubious about Roy, but so far all of his claims about Tom had rung true and despite his unorthodox way of going about things, it seemed that he had the potential to do something to stop this hideous gang of Saiful Das. Suddenly Roy stood and began to walk towards the door.

"Where are you going?" I called to him.

"To take these cards to the Police Office and begin to find out about any moneys moving. Strike while the iron is hot as you British say."

I started to try and move from my position on the floor to follow but another bolt of pain shot through my arm. I winced in agony.

"Please, Mrs Parker, you do not need to be getting up. The Police Station is only five minutes' walk away. It is most best if you are staying here. Outside are dangerous men who will be looking for you because of your husband and all of his dealings. If they see you outside in the street with me I may not be able to be keeping you safe. Here is the maximum safest place. Also," he looked around conspiratorially, even though it was only us in the small room and then dropped his voice to a whisper, "some of the policemen here are not to be trusted and may wish to be asking you many more questions about your husband. Not all of them will be as, ah, understanding as I have been about your part in all of this business." He marched up the stairs to the basement door, then turned, producing a key. "I will be locking this door just in case there is anyone who wishes to be causing harm to you. That way no one is entering and disturbing you. Be safe," he said, and in one swift movement he flashed me his manic grin and disappeared behind the stiff metal door which emitted a harsh squeal.

I sat immobile on the filthy floor listening to the sound of the key scratching in the lock before I was able to offer any word of argument. As I heard the bolt slam in the lock a sense of imprisonment besieged me and the capacity of the room seemed to halve in that single moment.

I suddenly became aware of Tom's body located no more than a metre in front of me and felt trapped in this room with the man who had so maliciously deceived me, insanely fearing that I would hear him move or breath, that he would now come to punish me for what I had discovered about him.

My senses were heightened by fear and without Roy's chatter the silence in the room became replaced with distant noises from outside. Every toot from a car horn or shrill cry from a street vendor made me jump and I expected to hear banging on the door as someone came to punish me for the crimes of my husband. I could hear my blood pumping in my ears and the beat did nothing to calm my fears. The sound of a road sweep's wiry brush scraping against the door caused me to leap up, placing my back against the wall like a wounded animal waiting to fend off an attack.

I placed my hand on my chest and tried to still my shuddering breaths and gain control of the situation. My mind was racing as I tried to hold on to any sort of intelligent thought process.

I had to trust Roy. It was as simple as that. I had to trust that he would return promptly and that by locking me in I would be safe. My stomach tightened as I thought about Roy and my misgivings about him, but after the revelations about Tom I felt that I should continue to hold back on my character assassinations. I prayed that on Roy's return I would have no more to endure, but would be free to go home.

*Home*. It was such a beautiful word that seemed so out of place here. I said it aloud to try and breathe life into it but it still remained an alien idea. Was it still possible to call where I had been home after everything that I had discovered on this journey? The whole life we had created together was just a lie and would never be the same, every memory tainted with deceit. Everything once precious to me was now lost.

A shout from outside the door drew me back to the present from my moment of self-pity. Right now survival was the most important thing. I had to sit back, remain calm and trust in Roy and his promises.

## Chapter Eighteen

*In all honesty, I was surprised that I had lasted this long without being revealed to the Madame in the brothel. Dipal had warned me that showing a photo of Aisha and asking questions would be risky, especially with the gossip in a kotha regardless of how much each girl was paid. I stood silently, waiting for her to tip her hand of knowledge so I could see if she had a full house or if I still had some bargaining power in the game.*

*"Do you not realise that all women in here are like sisters and I am like an auntie to them? In the showers, while cooking, eating, smoking, we are always talking, talking. Anything to make the time go quicker and* you," *she said, again stabbing me in the chest with her finger, "have been an area of great interest. Coming from nowhere, offering to bring business, asking lots of questions. Too many questions make you lose your tongue. You pay good money but don't touch the pretty girls. I hear it all. Dasji may be blinded by the money you are bringing in but I am not. I knew there was something different about you from the first time I was seeing you." She walked over and closed the door her voice becoming a whisper. "The girls tell me of the questions which you ask them. You are with the Police, yes?" she asked, her tone softening.*

*I slowly nodded my head, unable to think of another explanation. She sighed deeply.*

*"You may try to shut us down and maybe you will. But you close this kotha and another will rise, just as big on the other side of the city." She looked at me with sad eyes. "You know that as soon as you leave here it is my duty to tell Dasji all that I know?"*

*I nodded slowly again.*

*"He will kill you himself," she stated, not as a warning but as a simple fact. For a third time I nodded. She stood for a moment, uncertain. Then she raised the photo of Aisha to my face. "This girl, she is your daughter, yes?"*

*"Yes. Her name is Aisha," I stated, tears beginning to roll freely down my cheeks. "She was taken by Das."*

*"I cannot be imagining how that feels, though every day I see these girls. I have vowed never to have child myself as the pain of losing them to the brothel would be too much. I know you must judge me for the work I do, but I was once as these girls, sold by my parents to cover a debt and brought here. A few years ago I was given the option of continuing to satisfy men or to become the Madame, earning nearly five times as much." She shrugged, "what was I to do? I have learned to be hard to enforce rules but I try never to be cruel." She looked at me intently. "Within a month I knew this was your daughter from the way the girls spoke. You have shown great heart*

*trying to find her," she took my face in her hands. "You have the heart of a white tiger, but also you have teeth," she smiled sadly at me for a long moment, assessing me with her eyes. "I know where your daughter is," she stated.*

*I gasped, opening my mouth to ask a thousand questions but she held up her hand to still me.*

*"After you showed the picture, one of the girls, Nalini, told me all about what you had asked and shown her, scared it was a trap and that you were trying to get her in trouble. She had arrived about a week ago on the same truck as your daughter. She remembers teaching her songs and comforting her in the dark on the long journey from Agra. Your daughter was taken off with the other half off the girls to a brothel in Bowbazar. Nalini was then brought here."*

*The tragedy of the situation was not lost on me. Having searched so hard to find her, Aisha was now in touching distance but I was to be executed for having come so close. The tears continued to flow as I looked up at the Madame.*

*"Was she...ok?" I asked, unsure of how to phrase the question that I had wanted to know the answer to since the moment she was taken. The Madame nodded.*

*"Scared, but she has not been touched. She misses her Daddy." I exhaled gratefully.*

*"If only I could see her one last time..." I began but the Madame looked at me sternly.*

*"If I don't tell Das all I know then it will be me who is no more. You know how he will deal with a traitor,"* her eyes softened. *"There was a time when I was a small girl, no older than your daughter, running round in the fields of Ganjaheri, my village. I would hide in the long grass for hours pretending to be all sorts of wild animals. My favourite though was always the white tiger as it was rare and most beautiful. I always wanted to run free in the wild,"* she sighed. *"A few years later my Father was caught in a trap, and forced to cage me and sell me to Das, where I was placed forever in the concrete jungle no longer able to run free. I wish for those happy times as a child again, but they are now long gone."* She paused and looked at me, her eyes sparkling with tears. *"Your daughter has that chance to learn how to dream again. Let her take it,"* she urged me, placing her hands on my shoulders. *"I will not tell Dasji but I ask that when you carry out your raids and arrests that we may be left in peace here in Alankara Kotha. Do not tell anyone it was me who let you know."*

*I nodded, my heart ready to burst with gratitude. I pulled her close to me and embraced her, whispering my thanks in her ear. "I will never forget what you have done," I said.*

*"Go, now,"* she urged, *"do what you must. God be kind to you."*

*I smiled, hope burning away the dark clouds which had*

*covered my heart for so long. She smiled back at me, hair dishevelled, eyes teary, but a childlike smile on her face as I pictured her running through the long grass a million miles from here without a care in the world. That is how I chose to remember her, not as I saw her for the last time.*

*Sadly, God was not kind to us. We were both oblivious to the shadow of Roy lurking at the door.*

*In my excitement I ran obliviously past him to contact Dipal immediately. It took less than thirty minutes to be in his presence relaying all that I had been told by the Madame. A plan was formed to raid the brothel that evening. Normally raids would focus on arresting the girls involved in the sexual conduct, completely ignoring that they were usually forced into this practice. However, with the information, the photos, my testimony and catching Das and others in the act it would be possible to put them down for a long time. I would arrange to meet Das at the brothel in Bowbazar that evening on the promise of discussing business. Dipal and other Officers would raid it, arresting Das, his cronies and any paying customers. Roy would be exposed with my word and the photos we had collected, and a number of other raids would be carried out in all of the brothels in which I knew there were underage girls. The stash house where drugs were kept would also be raided, pulling off possibly one of the biggest raids in recent years and completely destroying Das while giving me back Aisha in the process.*

*I was giddy with excitement as Dipal left to arrange a team for that evening, blissfully unaware of the venomous snake that was Roy, waiting to pounce.*

*I arrived that evening in the lane by Bowbazar which Dipal had suggested. I saw him sitting in an old, grey Fiat with three other policemen. On the other side of the road was a similar car with another four police in civilian clothes. He nodded, giving the signal for me to progress towards the kotha. I pulled my coat tightly around me, thinking that as I left the kotha I could have Aisha in my arms as we walked away from this nightmare.*

*As I walked forwards the road seemed eerily quiet. I had visited this kotha on about three occasions and the street was normally vibrant with brightly dressed women lining the balconies and calling out to passing men, laughing and joking crudely, while spitting paan onto the street. Now though it appeared empty, my footsteps echoing on the wet street. I looked around nervously, my hope quickly being replaced with trepidation.*

*I approached the door to the kotha. It was silent as a tomb. I stepped inside and my eyes were drawn to a dark shape swinging from the roof above me. I squinted intently, trying to make it out, then suddenly there was an almighty crash and four police ran in through the back door, shouting their warnings in Hindi and flashing their torches around. The others, including Dipal, burst in through the front door in a similar manner, their spotlights all being drawn to one place.*

*The dark shape was now illuminated. The face of the Madame, her eyes open, staring at what I hoped was the long grasses of her village, hung from the roof, her body limp below her. She was completely naked, the word 'dēśadrōhī' or traitor etched across her body, the cuts still dripping with blood as we all stood silently staring for what seemed like an eternity before Dipal sprung back to life, ordering half the men to search the basement and the others to head to the upper floor.*

*He put an arm around me and tried supporting me as my body crumbled with grief and I slid to the floor, wringing my hands. It was all my fault. She had died at my asking and even worse was that she had died in vain. Her beautiful sacrifice had achieved nothing. My final resolve had gone and I sat there, inconsolable on the floor, her sticky blood wetting my trousers.*

*"Come," said Dipal, "you must move. We cannot stay here"*

*I looked at him. "You should lock me up. If it wasn't for me she would still be here." I said, unable to look at her body.*

*He shook his head. "There will be time to mourn and*

*grieve. Right now we have to get you as far from Kolkata as possible. Das must have been tipped off. If we don't, then this will be you next," he said pointing at the Madame, "and who knows, maybe me. Come, we must leave right now." With that he pulled me to my feet and pushed me in the direction of the door. "Go!" We began to jog back to the car, the other Police Officers still inside searching the building.*

*As soon as we were exposed in the middle of the street I heard the crack of a pistol being fired and a flash of light as it flew close to my ear, embedding itself in the wall on the other side of the road. I looked in the direction it had come from and saw about five faces I recognized from the weekly meetings, Das in the centre, his revolver drawn. "Traitor!" he screamed as he raised it to take a second shot.*

*Dipal grabbed my shirt, tugging me forward as I stood frozen to the spot. I stumbled after him, the shot narrowly missing me again. We sprinted forward, adrenaline pumping, shouts and the crack of guns following us down the empty street, sounding like bonfire night.*

*We sped off into the night, our threat contained by those police in the kotha. As the gun shots rang out I pleaded with Dipal to let me go back, to have my turn at Das but he refused, tearing away in the car as I tried to pull open the door which he had locked.*

*After months of planning, waiting, having patience, it was all over and once again the bad guys seemed to have won. I slumped down in my seat, defeated, as Dipal sped his way towards Kolkata airport.*

*As we arrived, I allowed Dipal to purchase me a ticket after arguing there was nothing more I could do now Das had the word out on me. Going anywhere near my apartment, Kolkata or even India would be suicide. That doesn't seem such a bad option right now, I thought.*

*On me were all the possessions I needed, my forged passport, some money, the photo of Aisha. I pulled out the photo of Sunita from my wallet and handed it to Dipal. "I'm sorry about your loss too. Seems that hope has left us." I extended my hand. "Thanks for everything, I really do appreciate it." He nodded humbly.*

*"Anything happens, and I mean anything, I will email you. As long as it is in my power, I will keep searching for Aisha. For now though, all you can do is head home."*

*"Home," I mused, "I have no idea what that means anymore."*

# Chapter Nineteen

A loud crash against the door paralysed me with fear and I sat and stared wide eyed for a full two minutes until I was assured that someone outside had just fallen into it, rather than a gang of perverts and murderers trying to break in and kill me. I closed my eyes and exhaled. I needed to calm down. I was jumping at shadows.

I slowly used my good arm to help me move from the ground and managed to get into a standing position without the pain consuming me. I tip toed over to Tom's body, somehow reasoning this would stop any potential murderers being able to hear me and come running. I leaned against the table, my head dizzy from a lack of food.

I steadied myself and looked down at the body of the stranger in front of me I had once called my husband. I felt like shaking him awake from his eternal slumber and screaming at him, showing him the trauma and pain his lies had brought to me. However, I was now unsure whether he would even care if he could have heard me.

I stared at his face until the raging storm of my emotions had subsided, leaving only a numb emptiness. I took his cold, rugged hand in mine for a final time, then slowly removed my wedding ring, my promise of eternal love, and placed it in his hand, pushing his fingers into a rigid fist.

As I lay his hand down, I noticed that his wedding ring was also missing. I caressed the back of his finger, rubbing over the indented flesh which look so naked without it. Had our marriage meant so little to him that he could just remove his ring and become another person without the ties and responsibilities it meant? Had he slipped in and out of character so easily, playing the role of loving husband one moment and child trafficker and murderer the next? Well, he had fooled me for long enough. Another passport for every day of the week. Who shall I be today? If something goes wrong I can just reinvent myself with a new tattoo and haircut!

"I really thought you loved me," I whispered into the silent body's waxy ear, "but you never even told me your real *name*. I gave you all, everything I had and you could just take it then slip it off when it suited you, just like your wedding ring. Cast aside. No wonder you didn't want any children. Just more responsibility to be forgotten when you had other business to attend to. Well, it's a good job we didn't have any in case they turned out like their Father," I said, my voice quivering. "I loved you. But no more. I will not cry for you," I said as I gathered up the grimy cloth sitting at his waist. I took one last look then pulled the sheet up over his face, covering him and the lies that seeped from his flesh, swearing that would be the last time I ever looked on him.

I flexed my left hand which now felt bare without the ring I had become so accustomed to wearing. Physically removing the ring let me almost feel like the connection between us had been broken and as if the guilt that I felt on me for Tom's actions had to some extent been dissolved.

As I stood by the blood splattered sheet I began to wonder what responsibility I had towards getting the body home. Was I meant to make the arrangements? How could I bring myself to get this corpse home knowing the damage he had wreaked in so many lives? All I wanted was to walk away from here and never think about him again, never even acknowledge that I once had a husband. If he had been able to so easily forget our marriage and his commitment to me, why should I have any further responsibility towards him? For all I cared the body could be cremated here and I could wash my hands of him and everything which he had done.

As I stood there by the table my concentration was broken as I heard the key scratching in the lock. I looked up fearfully as the door slowly creaked open. Behind it stood Roy, a small grin playing on his face as I cowered behind the table, anxiously waiting to see who had entered. I breathed a sigh of relief as he bounced down the steps, the grin remaining.

"What is the panic Mrs Parker?" he asked, "Did you not know it would be me? I told you it would only be being a short time," he said as he sauntered over towards me.

"I was worried it would be one of Das' gang," I confessed.

"But as I told you Mrs Parker, with me here you are being in the most safe place, his men will not hurt you. No harm can come to you now," he said, the grin still held, like one painted on a puppet.

"Did you manage to check the accounts? Had Tom transferred the money across?" I asked, curious to know what Roy had been doing all this time.

"Oh yes, I checked them Mrs Parker. I'm afraid that things are worse than I was first thinking. When was the last time you looked at this account?" he asked, pulling my card from his leather wallet like a magician displaying his tricks.

"I don't know, maybe a week ago," I replied, holding my hand out to receive back the card. He nodded his head gravely, but continued to hold the card out of my reach, like a child being taunted with sweets.

"I am afraid that since then your husband has made many transfers of cash into this account, much dirty money taken from his dealings with Das. This money has polluted the whole account, it is now impossible to tell what money was there before and if even that money was from these dealings in horrible crimes with the children. So, Mrs Parker, there was only one thing which I was able to be doing and that was to take all of the money out as evidence."

"What? But that is my entire life savings, it's all that I

have! I've saved for years into that account, and what, you just take it all? What am I supposed to do now? I can't even afford to get home!" I said, panic stricken.

"Getting home is something which you do not need to be worrying about," he said, the grin extending till it almost touched his ears, revealing his yellowed fangs. "The money will be here shortly, it will be brought by my associate," he said, drawing out the word. "I am sure that we can be thinking of some arrangement to make things more comfortable for you after all the trauma which you have faced but I am thinking that money is probably the least of your worries right now."

The back of my neck prickled at Roy's cloaked comments as I stood, my judgement clouded with anxiety and wondered what he meant and what would become of my entire life savings. Had I been a fool to trust him with my savings I pondered, or would the alternative have been worse? Had my savings been already used by Tom to fuel these sick exploits? Were they all tainted as Roy suggested. As I stood weighing up all these thoughts, Roy produced a new packet of cigarettes and proceeded to pull one from the packet. He casually struck a match and held it, the light flickering off of the middle finger on his left hand. A silver ring glimmering in the flame. Tom's wedding ring.

# Chapter Twenty

*I arrived back in Britain in a state of shell shock. Where I had once called home now seemed like an alien planet. The city of my birth made me feel like a stranger. It did not know my memories, it did not care for all I had lost. I wandered the cold streets feeling like I had been cut open, my organs removed and replaced with ice, my soul escaping in the process.*

*I stood for a moment outside Stansted airport watching a bright red balloon bouncing along the pavement, unaware to all that was around it, filled with nothing but air. It bounced along, oblivious, through the commuters, single mothers and drug addicts, never stopping, unmoved by them all. I felt a certain connection with it, seeing my life as meaningless as that balloon now that Aisha was lost. I watched it bounce further down the street till it landed on broken glass, popping, never to bounce again.*

*The next few weeks dragged by so slowly it felt as if time itself had stopped to mourn my loss, yet with my fingernails I still clung to the hope that I would soon hear from Dipal. That there may yet be news. Perhaps during the raids Aisha had been found. Maybe the Madame's death, the months of undercover work with those I despised, the selling of my soul had not all been in vain.*

*It took thirteen long, grey days before I finally received an email from Dipal. My final hopes all lay on the news it contained. I quickly read through his words-*

Dear Tom,

I am sorry for not writing sooner. It has been a most difficult time. Also, I have not known how to bring such cruel words to your already bruised heart.

During our raid in Bowbazar, Lal, an associate of Das, was shot and killed outside the brothel. However, two officers were also shot, one died instantly, the other is still in a serious condition. Das must have been informed about the other raids also. Only one of the brothels we got to was occupied with a number of young girls locked in the basement, which the Commissioner had deported but did nothing to the owners of the brothel or anyone else involved. The cocaine had been moved also. There was no sight of Aisha anywhere even after questioning.

With the raids revealing nothing and the death of an officer I was called before the Commissioner who has had me removed from the Police Force pending inquiry for a waste of Police time and money, and for not consulting the proper authorities before conducting such a raid. For this he has ignored all the evidence I have gathered on Das and without you or any other witnesses to speak against him the case is lost. I informed of all I knew on Roy but again the Commissioner made it very clear that my word and evidence were now inconsequential.

I am left with nothing and afraid that I am no more use to you or anyone. Forgive me for my failings. Hope is lost.

Your friend always,

Anthony Dipal

*That night, those words drove me to the top of a bridge over the A12. I stood for a few minutes, my feet inches from the edge as the traffic rushed by below. I closed my eyes, arms outstretched, swaying in the gentle breeze like a scarecrow. I felt weightless. All it would take was one small step, then like the balloon I would be gone, the blood of the sacrifices made by others no longer haunting me. "Hope is lost," I said, into the darkness, my words carried away on the engines of trucks hurtling past. I sighed. As enticing as nothingness was I knew I must continue, even if it was just to save someone the horror of discovering my body. I would remain a living ghost.*

*Over the next few months I became a pale reflection of even a ghost. With no one to care for, I cared not for myself. Despite having the money accumulated from my work with Das I slept on the streets welcoming the cold sting of the winter wind as part of my punishment for all that I had cost others. I was repulsed by all I had done and could find no escape from my shame. The bottom of a bottle was the only way to feel anything other than the crushing numbness that surrounded my heart. For months I was in this state, bitterness and regret taking root and destroying me from within. I became easily aggressive and trusted no one who tried to help or speak to me. It felt as if I were falling and gathering momentum with each instant that passed, unable and unwilling to do anything to try and stop my descent.*

*Eventually I hit the bottom. One freezing night I woke up in the local hospital, completely disorientated feeling like my inside had been scrubbed with a giant scourer covered in bleach. I asked the nurse through dry lips what had happened and she told me that I had just had my stomach pumped to remove the alcohol after being found half dead in a park by a mother and child. The girl had been so upset that she had not stopped crying even after the Paramedics had left she said reproachfully. I covered my eyes, ashamed, imagining Aisha having found me in that state. What would she think?*

*As I lay in the hospital bed that morning my mind was clear for the first time in months. It felt like a moment of epiphany. I had come close to the edge and realised that I was not ready to go over it yet. The words from the film Shawshank Redemption came repeatedly to my mind, 'get busy living or get busy dying.' I decided it was time to opt for the first and left the hospital determined to sort myself out and remember how it felt to be alive.*

*I was able to use the money I had left from my work with Das to help rent an apartment and provide food until I was able to get a job. I started to cook, to eat properly, to go running, to be clean, to search for jobs, to socialise. All of the time the loss of Aisha was there at the back of my mind but I knew that if by some miracle she was found I wanted to be someone who could look after her and love her. That drove me on every day, striving to be the man of which she would be proud.*

*I managed it. I was fit, healthy, working. I paid tax. I was a model citizen. But still, all I could feel was a numb sense of pain, joy still a forgotten emotion until about a year later, just as Christmas began to approach. I met you and you brought me back to life.*

# Chapter Twenty One

Roy inhaled deeply, sighing with pleasure as he exhaled. I stood stunned, studying the silver ring on his finger which I had given to my husband on the day of our wedding. It was far too large and looked completely out of place on Roy's stained fingers. He looked at me, then followed my gaze to his finger. He smiled then held up his bony hand for me to study.

"That's Tom's ring," I stated, in disbelief.

"That is correct Mrs. Parker," he retorted, continuing to puff on his cigarette.

"But, why have you got it?"

"Because I took it from his body when I killed him."

# Chapter Twenty Two

*Life had become like a black and white movie to which you brought colour and reminded me there was more than just continued existence. You taught me that it could be enjoyed again. You showed me why a million songs are written about love and why despite the numerous clichés, it is the most amazing thing in the world. Somehow you found it in your pure, beautiful heart to make room for me and my wounded, calloused soul. You were amazing and you still are. Every moment with you I feel like a ghost returning to earth having been denied joy and being given an unexpected and glorious second chance.*

*I know that so often I put up walls between us with my lies and I am so sorry that I did not tell you all of this before as you were the only one who ever accepted me. My pride so often got in the way of what we had but I have to tell you how much I need you. As I am on this flight writing now, the only thing which gives me the courage to continue is the thought of coming back to you and seeing you smile once more. To hold you in my arms and tell you that I love you. I pray that it will be with Aisha, that at last you will have the family which I was unable to give you.*

*I know there is no justification for my lies but after all the pain suffered, I somehow reasoned in my superstitious mind that if I told you these things somehow something terrible would happen to us, so I buried them deep, hoping that they would stay there forever.*

*Knowing that you are safe now will be what drives me on, regardless of what dangers I face when I leave the plane.*

## Chapter Twenty Three

I stood, silently staring at Roy, my mouth wide open in shock as the hairs on the back of my neck rose and tingled. A prickling sensation ran through my body as I gasped for breath. Subconsciously I stepped backwards, arms raised before me shaking my head.

"You? You? All this time... but, what..." I stuttered, struggling to form the words I needed to. Roy stood motionless, continuing to drag on his cigarette as if he had just commented on the weather.

"Come now Mrs Parker. This can be coming as no big surprises to you. I have already told you what kind of man was your husband and as someone to be keeping the law it was only natural we would be coming to some strong disagreements. I can be assuring you he did not suffer in the killing, very much," he said, the side of his mouth flickering into a smile as he took a step towards me. "Just as you will not be to suffer much," he said as he continued to advance slowly towards me, one hand hovering by his revolver.

In a state of panic and confusion I tried to run backwards, but toppled over my own feet, landing awkwardly and becoming momentarily blinded by the pain. I cried out in agony and desperation as Roy came and stood over me, arms now folded as he looked down at me and laughed.

"Mrs Parker, there is no point in crying out here, no one is able to be hearing a word of it. If you are being in pain then I will be most glad to be helping you out of it." He began to reach over to grab me around the neck. Instinctively I fell further on my back to distance myself from him, feeling the broken chair leg pushing into my arm. Instinctively I grabbed it, swinging as hard as I could at Roy's face, catching him just below his ear on the neck. He crumpled on the ground next to me, emitting a small moan as he fell.

This was an opportunity I had to seize. My pain was dulled by adrenaline as I rolled over, looking at the door and knowing if I could just get that far that the crowded streets would provide safety. I scrambled to my feet and was about to step forward when Roy hooked his ankle around mine, sending me sprawling again. He was quickest to his feet this time, holding his neck with one hand as he cursed at me in Hindi. I reached out my arm again to grab the chair leg which had fallen just in front of me but Roy was too fast, stamping down hard on my hand and holding it pressed to the ground under his heavy boots as I yelped in pain. His other boot he placed on my throat, slowly increasing the pressure on my trachea, choking the life from me. I flailed my legs around helplessly, luckily managing to catch him just behind his other knee, causing his leg to buckle and giving me an opportunity to roll free.

However, he was too fast for me and jumped on my back like a hyena sensing its prey weakening. He grabbed my hair, pulling my head helplessly back, forcing me to look into his grinning face that was shining with sweat. "Maybe you will be seeing your husband sooner than you are thinking," he grunted.

My throat was dry but somehow I managed to muster enough saliva to spit directly in his eye, causing him to momentarily let go off me as his arms flew to his face to try and alleviate his temporary blindness. He left his torso completely open and I saw the barrel of the revolver twinkling at me. I snatched at it, managing in one swift movement to dislodge it from his belt, but was surprised at the weight it carried. It fell from my hand, bouncing off of the floor emitting a loud crack as the gun fired, blinding me with a burst of light.

For a second we were both held in stunned silence, then almost as if it was synchronised we both dived for the gun. I managed to get my fingers to it first, clawing it towards me, but Roy was too strong and managed to grab my arm before I could direct it towards him. We rolled on the floor, my arms tensed away from my body as Roy tried to force the gun from my hands. Two shots rang out in quick succession, the bullets ricocheting around the room. I heard Roy cry out and he released me, falling backwards on to the ground, clutching his side as claret began to fill his hand. He gasped, looking at me in shock, his eyes wide like a frightened child. I looked back, revolver held at my waist, an equally shocked expression on my face.

Slowly I pulled the gun up so that it was pointed at his chest, both hands shaking as they held it tightly. He looked back at me helplessly, gasping for breath, his eyes pleading.

"You... are... not... a... murderer, Mrs Parker," he wheezed, having to say a word at a time as he grimaced with the effort of speaking. How badly he was wounded I had no idea but blood was running through his fingers and slowly dripping onto the ground, mixing with the dust.

"You don't know me," I said, "and you don't know what I'm capable of. You took my husband away from me! My husband!"

"I... know... that you... are not... capable... of taking... a life. The... guilt," he shook his head as he managed to heave himself into an upright position.

I stood, still shaking, the gun pointed at Roy.

"Give... me the... gun," he said, holding out a bloodied hand, "or... shoot," he said, shrugging. Still I hesitated, hatred welling up inside of me, but something holding me back, even after all he had done. Was it pity as he sat at my mercy?

He snorted. "Coward. Just-like-your-husband," and he began to push himself slowly to his feet. I knew it was now or never. He began to straighten up.

"Stay where you are," I commanded, waving the gun at him. He chuckled and took an unsteady step forward. "Stay there!" I shouted, and he looked at me, staggering forward another uncertain step, still clutching his side. I gripped the gun even more tightly, feeling like it would buckle under the pressure. I placed a finger on the trigger and held it for what seemed like an eternity.

Roy took another step, raising his arm.

Using all my strength for such a small job I squeezed the trigger, closing my eyes as I prepared for the crack of the bullet.

An empty click.

Roy laughed and took another step. I opened my eyes, startled and pressed it again. Still only a click. It was out of bullets. Roy continued to advance on me like a zombie, one arm covering his side, the other raised in front of him as the blood on his shirt slowly spread.

I cursed, then moved around the table, trying to put as much distance as possible between Roy and myself. He stood on one side, I was on the other, Tom's body on the table was all that separated us. The shot did not look like it would be fatal but it had slowed him down. I now had the advantage of speed, though every step made me wince with pain. I moved one way then the other, Roy copying me as if we were in a mirror. Then, summoning all of my strength, I darted for the door, blocking out the pain as best as possible. I grabbed the handle and pulled. Nothing. I pulled again. It did not budge an inch. In frustration I kicked hard at it in desperation, hurting my foot in the process.

Turning round I saw Roy still standing by the table, a wide grin plastered on his face. In his hand he dangled the key between two blood soaked fingers. "I am thinking... you may have... forgotten something," he chuckled between breaths.

"Give me the key!" I shouted.

He chuckled again. "I am afraid... that is... not what... will be happe... ning" he said, placing it back in his top pocket and tapping it gleefully. "If you want it... come and get it." He leaned on the table for support, eyes ablaze.

I considered my options. Despite his injury Roy would probably still be able to overpower me and I feared getting near him. Like a wounded animal he was now at his most dangerous. However, he would need treatment soon. Even if the wound was not too serious, he was still bleeding fairly heavily.

"You need to get to hospital," I reasoned. "If not, you won't survive. You give me the key and I'll go and get help. We both live, I will disappear and you can carry on doing whatever it is you do. If not, I wait for you to bleed to death, then take the key and escape anyway. Your choice, I've got a lot longer than you," I said, sitting down on the step next to the door to emphasise my point. He slowly lowered himself on to the floor, raising his shirt to inspect his wound. He winced, then gingerly removed the shirt, tying it around his waist to stem the bleeding. He closed his eyes and breathed deeply with the effort, placing the key from his pocket on the floor next to him. He sat for a moment, unmoving apart from the rise and fall of his chest. I wondered if he was losing consciousness, considering if I should creep up and take the key.

With his eyes still closed the sly grin returned to his face as loud steps were heard outside the door. "There is... something which... you have forgotten... Mrs... Parker." A key scraped in the lock and then the door squeaked open.

# Chapter Twenty Four

*Then, a few days ago, after so many years of uncertainty and assuming Aisha was dead or would never be found, I received another email from Dipal, like a ghost from the past.*

My dear friend,

I am sorry for my long silence. Shame has stopped me contacting you these seven years. As you know, I no longer work for the police, but have been forced to become a street sweeper as I have been unable to get another job as a Dalit. Times have been hard and I now stay on the floor of a shop in which another four or five men sleep for a small amount of rent. However, I do not write to tell you of my misfortune. I bring you news. One of these men has just started driving trucks for Das. A wiry, nothing man who chews paan and talks too fast and too often. He often boasts of his contacts and the women he has been with. He recently returned from Uttar Pradesh after picking up a number of girls. He sat and talked to those who would listen about the women in the truck and one who he had forced himself upon as if it was a great achievement.

He mentioned that there was one young girl on the truck just like Aishwarya Rai. Big emerald green eyes and pale skin, maybe eleven, twelve years old. He was too scared to touch her as Das had specifically mentioned that she was a virgin and would make lots of money for him but that did not stop him talking about her. He was willing to speak and told me straight away which kotha she had been taken too and the new name she had been given, aṅgrējī gulāba, meaning English rose. Immediately I thought of Aisha, but cannot visit the kotha for fear that I will be recognised and she will be moved.

I wanted immediately to give you this report. I am unsure it is her, but I feel in my heart that it is. Hope has returned like a beautiful bird after a cold, dark, winter.

If you can come, tell me when and once more we shall be united to save your daughter.

Your friend always,

Anthony Dipal

*As you now know I told you I was leaving for a business trip and the very next day left for Kolkata. Right now I'm on the plane, preparing for what is ahead. I wanted desperately to share with you then all that had happened but feared you may have stopped me due to the danger, or worse still, that you may have left me. So I sit here now, alone, with so many questions in my mind. Is it Aisha? Will she recognise me? How can I rescue her? Will I see Das? I am pondering this final question at the moment, knowing somehow I will, almost willing it so that I will have the opportunity to slay the beast which has covered the land in darkness for so long.*

*I hope that as you read this letter I may be by your side, Aisha also there to complete us. If I am not, then I fear either you will no longer speak to me or something may have gone wrong on this mission, be it prison or death, either of which I would willingly accept to free Aisha. If so I ask for understanding even if forgiveness is not possible.*

*My darling, I wish I could have been better and been the man you deserve. I pray that I may have a second chance to be that man. I love you with all my heart.*

*Yours forever,*

*Tom x x x*

# Chapter Twenty Five

I sat, unable to move, looking up at the enormous stomach of the suited figure looming above me, a sports bag tossed casually over his shoulder. His huge hands, rolls of fat and dead eyes all looked remarkably familiar. It took a second to recall where I had seen him and then suddenly I gasped.

Das.

He pushed the door hard behind him, the loud bang echoing around the room, then without a word his eyes fluttered between a thankful Roy, slouched and bloodied on the floor and me sitting at his feet stupefied. In an instant he took in the appearance of Roy and the revolver resting in my hand on my knee. In one step he had closed the gap between us and kicked the revolver free from my hand, sending it scuttling across the floor with far more speed or agility than denotes a man of his size. He then stood towering above me, arms folded on his stomach as he shouted across the room to Roy in Hindi, nodding every now and again. Roy looked at his side a number of times and seemed to be saying that he was OK.

That business dealt with, without a word he reached down and grabbed me by the hair and dragged me kicking and screaming across the room towards the table. I tried to strike at him but my hands just bounced off like a small child having an outburst. Once there, he held both my hands in one of his, the pressure alone feeling like it would crush them. With his spare hand he fished around inside the sports bag, quickly withdrawing a knotted rope, with which he tightly bound my arms behind my back, joining them to the table to prevent me trying to move.

Roy slouched just a few feet away from me and watched every move before turning to face me. "May I introduce... a dear friend of mine... Saiful Das."

Das stood back looking at me, breathing deeply at the exertion of the previous few minutes. He then squatted down so that his face was level with mine.

"Your husband was a filthy traitor," he stated, letting the words fall heavily from his tongue.

"You are a filthy, murdering, child selling..." he slapped me hard across the face, almost dislocating my jaw.

"I have not asked you to speak. When I am asking then you may. Understand?" he asked. I kept my eyes turned down, trying to blink back my tears. He grabbed my face in his vast hand and jerked my chin up towards him. "I said, understand?"

This time I nodded as much as possible in the vice like grip with which he held me.

"Good, then we will be getting on very nicely," he said, smiling at me sarcastically, his face inches from mine, the smell of whisky burning my nostrils as he breathed heavily on me. He released me then turned his attention to Roy, this time continuing to speak in English. "What did she know?" Roy shook his head, "nothing... she knew nothing... not about...any of it. Even after threats."

Das nodded his head, mulling over the information he had just received. "And you picked her up from the airport as we discussed?" Again, Roy nodded his head in agreeance. "Any children? Does anyone know that she is here?" Roy shook his head. "No one at all. She is... all alone. Completely alone."

"Good, very good," he turned his attention back towards me. "You see, your husband has been here, causing many problems for me and my friends. As I am sure Superintendent Roy has been telling you, I am a business man who used to be working with your husband many years ago."

"Business?" I snorted in disgust, "what sort of business is that?" He slapped me hard again.

"How many times will I be telling you? Do not speak until you are being asked. Now, as I was saying, I run a business, transporting women around the country for sex making very many men very happy." He read my sickened expression and continued. "These girls I own, buy or steal, they are all looked after nicely. Put in kothas, protected so no one is hurting them, they are very expensive and if I am not giving them jobs what will they do? Begging? Rag collecting? Ha! They make ten times more with me."

I held my tongue, fearful of angering him.

"Big business, I am head of it all, make sure it all runs smoothly. I make more money every year than doctors, bank men, sports stars!" As he spoke about himself his pride began to swell. "Thousands of girls around the country, all bringing me takings through the sex trade. Cocaine too. Buying and selling. Big prices," he reached into his sports bag, pulling out a large packet of white powder, while exposing many more packets of the same, covered in numerous books, sheets of paper and stacks of money.

"Your husband, for a time, I am thinking is very good businessman for me. I give him trust, treat him like a son and then he turns on me like a snake," he looked away and spat at the ground. "Now, many years later he comes back and visits my brothel, trying to steal girls and take my money. He brings police onto my back. This is why I am carrying this," he said, shaking the sports bag, "to be avoiding trouble with police." He pulled out one of the books. "Very dangerous carrying all these drugs and books here with girls names, prices, which brothel they are working. He alert the police and they are looking for me for short time so I have to leave and keep these hidden." He saw my eyes drifting to the stacks of money. He smiled his gold toothed grin at me as he ran his hand through the notes affectionately. "These are the one good thing to come from your husband and thanking to you and your American visa," he laughed. The irony of my stupidity was not lost on me that I had allowed Roy to withdraw the money from our account to stop it going to child trafficking and in the process it had ended up right in the pocket of Das. I closed my eyes, feeling an idiot.

"Your husband was talking too much to police and this is how he brings trouble to me. That's why he ends up dead on a table. You see, problem with him talking is I do not know how much he is knowing. He disappears for many years, finds pretty wife and who knows what evidence he has at home about our business, about certain police officers," he says, motioning to Roy. "This can all be very bad news for us. That's why when he come back and dies I told Roy to call you so you can come over and we can know if he has spread stories at home which might give us problems. Luckily you are able to be coming over here and clear this up for us that he is very secretive and has kept these things quiet with no one else knowing things. This means he kept it all to himself, so if I am disappearing for a short while there will be no more problems and soon I can come back and carry on my business. Everybody is now happy." He tapped his fingers on his chin, then in mock surprise said, "but wait! There is now one problem! You now know too much and may be talking, talking to police like your husband," he covered his chubby mouth with his hand, pretending to gasp. I shook my head quickly.

"Please, if you let me go I won't say anything to anyone. I will..." I began but was cut off as Das raised his hand, whether for silence or to slap me I'm not sure. He looked me in the eye again.

"You are the problem which must now be taken care of," he said, reaching inside his jacket to produce a gun. He cocked it, then looked at Roy and his bleeding side.

"Perhaps, you would be liking to take this shot?" he asked as he passed the gun to Roy. Roy took it in his bloodied hand and shaking slightly pointed it at my chest.

"With pleasure," he grinned.

# Chapter Twenty Six

"My name is aṅgrējī gulāba," I said quietly in Hindi, breaking the silence. I sat for a moment, gently stroking the green and pink rakhi on my arm for comfort while looking at the ground. "I don't like my name. I used to have another name. A prettier name. I was called Aisha but that feels like it was a million years ago." I pointed to the door of the cellar towards the men who had brought us to this prison. "They gave me a new name. Said that I was never to use my old name again because it was dirty. I had a new name for a new city." I looked up at the other faces in front of me. The room we were in was very small, even smaller than the kitchen where I used to make chapatti's and rice for the ladies who were working. I used to sleep there too, but it was very hot and I would lie awake counting the cockroaches and trying to ignore the whirr of their wings.

Me and the other girls arrived here late last night when it was dark and we were given a blanket each. We had not eaten after being on the truck for a long time and we were given a small bowl of rice each which tasted so good because we were very hungry. The Madame here has a very strict face and hit a few of the girls for leaving the truck too slowly. I am scared that she will hit me too so I try to do everything as quickly as I can.

Before I was in another place like this. I was there for a long time. It was not a very nice place to work. Every morning I would have to get up early and wash the saris of all the women who were working there. I would have to wash them all with my hands in water that made my fingers go sore and cracked like an old lady. I did not mind working early though because it was the only time it was quiet. Apart from that it was always noisy. People talking, drinking, shouting, making love noises as the Madame called them. It did not sound like love though with the screams and grunts, it sounded like the pigs which were outside the kotha chewing on the rubbish we threw away.

My favourite part of the day was after I finished washing. I would have to go to the roof of the kotha and hang out the saris on the rooftop to dry. Shcila would come to help me. She was the same age and we would work very slowly, enjoying feeling the sun on our faces after days only in the dark and smoke. Sometimes we would play games and dance, using the saris to pretend that we were film stars, holding them in front of our faces as they dried on the line and singing songs from all the films which we heard from some of the ladies rooms and from radios outside. Sheila would sometimes say to me that I looked like a famous actresses like Aishwarya Rai and make me go hot in the cheeks. I knew that someone as beautiful as her would never work in a place like this.

Often the Madame would come up to see what was taking us so long and we would go straight back to work, pretending that we had been working hard all along, smiling in our secret when the Madame's back was turned. She was a kind lady though, unlike a few of the Madame's who I worked for when I was very young. I had seen girls brought in when I was only a small child and she would beat them in front of me because they did not want to work. Others would call me names or make jokes about my parents because of my green eyes. This one was strict but sometimes during big festivals like Divali she would bring sweets to me and the younger girls. Sometimes she would even give me a few rupees to run to the market to buy her fruit.

From the late morning though the ladies began waking up and shouting at each other, bickering about who made most money and had the biggest room. I had to work in the kitchen making them chappati's and chai. When I first started I burned myself a few times because I had not made them before and the big pot for the chai was very hot and really heavy. There were no windows though and I was not given a fan like some of the ladies had in their rooms. I did not complain because one of the girls did and her job now was cleaning the toilets.

In the evening I would collect money from some of the men and take them to the women in their rooms then give the money straight to the Madame. Anyone caught stealing would be hit with a belt. One of the girls did once and she could not sit down for at least a week. She showed us all the marks it left on her.

I did not like the men who would visit. They would all have a face like they were very important people and you were dirty. When they talked to me and the ladies they would always look all over your body and not look you in your eyes when they spoke to you. It was like they were trying to see through everyone's clothes. Sometimes they would try and touch me but the Madame was normally around and would give them a hard slap. I liked it when she did that. It felt like she was my Mum protecting me.

I think my real mum died when I was just a baby. I remember daddy saying she was not around anymore. I miss my Dad. He was always kind and fun. We used to live together, me, him and a nice lady who cooked food for us but I cannot remember her name. I was only small then. I remember with Dad I was allowed to go to the market whenever I wanted and sometimes he would buy me presents like a new dress or toys. Here the only new clothes I get are the ones which no one else wants anymore and they are always too big.

I can't remember much more about my Dad though, I have not seen him in many years, since the day at the market that some men came and took me away. One minute I was with him and then the next I had been carried away and put in a car. A few days later I remember I was taken somewhere in a truck and then I began sleeping in kitchens and living in the kotha's, always surrounded by lots of people. I don't know how long ago that was, I'm not even sure how old I am but I think about eleven because I am the same size as a few girls that age. The saddest thing for me is that I can't even remember what my Dad looked like. I don't have any photos. Some days I cry because I miss him and other days I imagine he is going to come and find me and take me back to our house where only we live and there are no more strange men or Madame's. I really hope that I will see him again.

"My name is Parvati," the girl on my right said. We had all been picked up and put on a truck and carried for hours but this was the first time that any of us had spoken. We had been too scared on the truck with one man always left in the back watching us. At one point he had torn off the kameez of one of the girls and laughed as she cried and tried to cover her naked chest. When we had arrived we were still too scared and nervous in the darkness, but this morning the small chink of light coming through the bottom of the door made us a little braver to talk. "I am sixteen. I am from a village near Lucknow. My father is a farmer. Last year his crops failed and our animals died of some disease. He borrowed a lot of money from a man who visits the village. We hoped that we would buy extra crops and animals but this year the crops did not grow again and the animals again are sick. My Father could not pay back the money to the man so a few days ago he came to our village and told my Father that either me or my brother would have to go with him to work until the debt was paid off. My brother is in school so I was sent. They said that I will be taken home when I have made enough money, but when we arrived last night he said I now owe him more money because he gave me transport here and food. I do not know what kind of work they will make me do."

When Parvati had said this we all sat silently, most of us already had been working in kotha's and knew more of what we would do. I had done lots of work washing and cooking so I guessed that's what I would be doing, but I knew that in the other kothas all the older girls had a very different work with the men at night. No-one wanted to tell Parvati.

"My name is Minu," a girl across the room said into the silence. "I am eighteen. Two years ago I lived in Lucknow and was at school. The very best in my class. My teacher was even telling me about different Universities. I was wanting to study Politics. In my spare time I would work as a waitress in a restaurant, taking food to customers so that I could save up money for University as my Father was not very rich. When I was working a handsome man used to come in and eat, often leaving me lots of rupees as a tip. I would always smile and thank him, delighted at his generosity. After a few weeks he began to come in more regularly and would start to leave small presents for me, one day even leaving a beautiful pair of earrings.

I was young and stupid. Forgetting my modesty I would linger at his table and talk with him. He told me he was visiting from Delhi and that he was a rich business man there. I told him of my dreams to go to University and study Politics. He invited me to come with him for a few days to Delhi to see the wonderful Universities and the Red Fort. I was charmed and agreed, telling my Father that I was staying at a friend's for the weekend. However, the Delhi I saw was one very different to that which was promised. I was led through bazaars and markets and taken to a building which he said his sister owned. He took me in and introduced me to her, then left me there saying he had urgent business to attend to and he would be back soon.

I never saw him again.

The lady was a Madame. In the beginning she treated me kindly, asking if I was OK, feeding me well and not letting anyone else in to see me. She gave me a bed, a new sari and some make up and would try and cheer me as I worried what may have happened to him.

I was stuck alone in a foreign city though as they had

planned between them and it was not long until the Madame's generosity was held over me as money which I owed her. Things she had given me as gifts were now things I had to pay her back for.

She introduced me to the other girls and showed me how to please a man. I did not want to but I had never travelled alone and had no money to escape. At first I refused to do it and the Madame wiped chili powder on my eyes. Soon I had to give in, fearing what else she may do."

Minu stopped for a minute and wiped her eyes.

"At first it was very painful and difficult but the Madame only allowed one man an evening to be with me. Soon though she said I was not bringing her enough money and I had to work harder. Just before I was put on the truck to come here she would send up to ten men a night to my room and I would not see a rupee because she said I still owed her money."

A few of the other girls gasped, including Parvarti as they began to realize what a horrible place we had been taken to. Parvarti began to cry and I reached out my hand to her in the dark. Minu sat and stared straight ahead. "I hope that we may be treated better here," she offered hopefully. Again we all became silent, Parvarti's story leaving even the girls who had been in the kothas for a while sad and scared.

Suddenly we heard big feet walking past the door and blocking out the light so we were in complete darkness. I felt

Minu squeeze my hand. I squeezed her hand too, scared of what was to happen next. Luckily the feet kept walking. All the girls breathed out together, like we were all one giant body with only one mouth.

"I am Keva," another girl spoke up once we knew we were alone again. "I am sixteen." She spoke slowly with a very strong Nepali accent, making it difficult to know what she was saying. She was the girl the man had touched in the truck. She did not look up as she spoke like the other girls. "I am from Nepal. A very poor family. Man promises me good job here. Teaching Nepali children. Good wage. House to live." She shrugged her shoulders and then became quiet again, all of us understanding how she felt without her saying another word. She pulled her blanket over her face and disappeared into the darkness, sobbing softly.

"I am Kareena," a girl to my left said in a loud voice. She had sat near me in the truck and was probably even younger than me. She was definitely shorter and had fat cheeks like a child. "It's easy to remember because it is the same as Kareena Kapoor. People say that I look like her," she said proudly. A few of the girls in the room smiled. "When I grow up I am going to be just like her and marry a famous Bollywood actor like Shahrukh Kahn. He is the best one. But he is a bit old now," she said, a hint of sadness in her voice. "I am nine years old but I will be ten soon. My dad said I had to go with the man in the truck because he owed him lots of money. He said that I would be home soon but I didn't believe him because he was crying when he said it. I didn't want to go with the man in the truck. He had red teeth and stank like dad when he drinks too much and wakes up angry in the mornings and he had a mean face like this," she said, sticking out her teeth and making her eyes meet in the middle.

This time all the girls smiled and a few even laughed. It seemed a funny noise to hear laughing in this dark room. "I bet he doesn't have a wife and that's why he is so mean to everyone. Dad used to say that about all the men in the village who didn't have a wife," she paused to think, and then scratched her head. "He used to say that the men who were grumpy and married were like that because of their wives too though," she shrugged to show that she did not understand, then continued to speak. "I used to live in the countryside and it was much nicer than this room here. I could run around everywhere and do whatever I wanted as long as I got water from the well and fed the animals."

After being quiet for so long it was really nice to hear Kareena speaking. The dark did not feel as scary when she was speaking. If I closed my eyes and listened to her I could almost imagine what it looked like on her farm. That made me smile.

"Me and some of the other girls in the village used to hide

in the long grass by the river. We would tell stories and jokes to pass the time. I knew the most jokes and the funniest ones because my brother Dev would tell me them and he was three years older so he knew some rude ones. I bet some of them would even make that mean truck driver laugh!" she said, giggling.

We all smiled too and I felt like we were in that long grass hiding, safe away from everything else. For about the next ten minutes Kareena chatted away, telling us about where she was from and sometimes taking a breath to ask someone else a question. She began pretending to be the truck driver again when suddenly the door at the top was pushed open. The sunlight burst in and we all became silent and closed our eyes because it was too bright. We covered our eyes so we could see what was happening.

At the top of the stairs was the really fat man. I could only see his shadow but I knew it was him because he was the fattest man I have ever seen. The day after I had been taken by the men at the market he had come to see me and said that he was family now but I did not want him as my family. He had a big stick he would hit the girls with but he told the Madame that no-one was to hit me because I had to be perfect. He was horrible and scary and always smelt like smoke. His name was Das but Sheila and me used to call him fat man because he was so fat, but only when we were alone.

He stood there for a minute with his hands on his hips and I think he was looking at us but I couldn't see because he was mostly a shadow and also because for some reason he was wearing a pair of sunglasses even though he was not a film star.

A number of shadows appeared at the fat man's side. They all walked a few steps down so that they were on the same level as all of us and we could see them. The fat man looked at us and smiled. He had a mouth full of golden teeth. All of us moved back as far as we could, scared of what he would do. He walked over and pulled Minu to her feet by her arms. She was shaking. He pulled open her mouth with his huge fingers and looked at her teeth, nodding as he did so. He clicked his fingers and one of the men came and carried her upstairs. She went without saying a word. We all watched in silence wondering if it would be us next.

He paced around the room, stopping in front of every girl and looking at them in the same way. Sometimes he would stop and say something, normally, 'very nice.'

When he came to Keva he shook his head and turned to one of the men angrily, "too dark." One of the men came and took her by the arm, grabbing her hard. She cried out as she was taken up the stairs.

The rest of the girls he looked at then he placed his big, fat feet in front of me. He bent over and put his face almost next to mine. He was sweating a lot and smelt sickly sweet like a lot of the men in the kotha's did. "Look at those eyes," he said, loudly in Hindi, pulling my face towards him so he could see me better. "Still so beautiful. You will make me a lot of money. In fact, you will begin making me money tomorrow night," he said as he laughed. "Tonight you will be with Karuna, the Madame. She will tell you all that you need to know to start work."

I had been working since I was about five with cleaning and cooking so I did not know what else the Madame would need to be telling me. I felt nervous as he held out his hand to help me to my feet. My hand felt tiny in his. Unlike Minu and Keva he helped me up gently. "You will be the diamond in our kotha, bringing many men. We already have one who has paid special big price for your innocence."

# Chapter Twenty Seven

I was chained up, exhausted, in excruciating pain and everything I had once held precious had been yanked away from me leaving me completely distraught. Yet as I stared at Roy with the revolver pointed at my chest my will to live became so strong that the adrenaline covered all pain like morphine. I could not give these scumbags the satisfaction of quietly doing away with me as if I had not existed. I had to survive even if it was just to spite them. Any extra moment of life I could buy was a beautiful victory.

I frantically scanned the room for inspiration to stall the impending shot as Roy raised his other hand to steady the gun. They searched the bare walls, the grinning face of Das, the gnarled table and then fell on Das' bag, money and cocaine spilling from it.

"Any-final-words?" he grunted, spitting on the dusty ground.

"I can get you more money!" I blurted out, half hysterical as the gun seemed to swell in size until it was all that filled my vision. Roy cackled at my desperation and flicked the safety off with his finger, continuing to hold me in the firing line. However, Das held his hand in front of Roy, his eyes trained on me. "Speak," he instructed me.

"She lies. Just like… her husband. She already gave me-all

her cards," Roy began to say.

Das barked at him, "cupa rahō. I asked her, not you. Where is this money?" he spat as Roy glared at him, the gun now nestling in his lap. I could feel the unspoken tension and resentment between the two men and decided to try and press this advantage for lack of a better plan, hoping that somehow along the way I would discover a way to freedom. Though Roy held the gun I could see that Das was the man who gave the orders so I decided to try and turn the men on each other, hoping they would devour each other like the wolves that they were.

"I see that you already have taken the ten thousand from my account with Tom," I said motioning to the bag on the floor with my head. I knew that we had under five thousand in the account but hoped that Das would be fooled by my bluff. "I also have," I began, praying that Das would intervene. Shrewd as ever his face darkened and he narrowed his eyes at Roy.

"Ten thousand?" he asked, and I nodded. "Ten thousand?" he said to Roy, his face contorting in rage. Roy looked at me, his face dismayed as he suddenly realized what I had done.

"Liar!" he screamed, pulling the revolver up with all the speed he could muster, but with his injury he was far too sluggish. Das pre-empted the danger and kicked the gun clear of his body. Roy yelped in pain then looked at Das, his eyes full of panic. "There was only-five thousand! She lies!" he panted, folding his hands into his armpits in an attempt to abate the throbbing.

"Even now you lie to me," Das retorted, wringing his hands in rage.

"She is the liar!" he said, wriggling away from Das as he spoke, leaving a small trail of blood, much like the residue of a snail. Das reached over, picking up the revolver.

"Her husband lied to you! So is she!" he squealed in terror. Das seemed to take a moment to consider this then nodded his ascent and brought the gun up to my eye level. I closed my eyes, waiting for death to come and take me from this place.

I heard the clap of the gun, the noise deafening, but felt nothing. Maybe it would be painless after all.

After a long moment I opened my eyes and looked up to see Das still staring at me, his eyes crazed as the gun pointed towards the floor, blue smoke slowly wafting out. Roy was slumped over, a hole in his chest, in a similar position to the fatal wound he had given Tom. A bubble of blood escaped his mouth as he stared wide eyed and unmoving at the stained ceiling as if studying it intensely.

I blinked in astonishment, unsure of what I was seeing. Das took a step closer, making sure he had my full attention. "You will get me more money. If not," he waved the gun at Roy's body, "you will be next."

## Chapter Twenty Eight

For the first time since I was very small I had my own room with a bed. I even had a fan which spun around quickly on the ceiling like a helicopter. There were no cockroaches or rats climbing the walls. I had my own blanket and a big, soft pillow, but even with all this I did not sleep at all on my first night in the kotha.

The fat man had taken me up the stairs and had introduced me to the Madame. I did not like him and his shiny gold teeth at all. When he put a hand on me it felt like a cockroach crawling on my skin. I made sure I did not say anything though because he could squash me into the ground like an ant in one step under his gigantic feet.

The Madame was prettier in the sunlight. After being so mean and hitting the girls on the way out of the truck she smiled lots at me, almost is if she was paid to smile. She led me through the maze of the kotha, an arm around me as we walked past women wearing bright red lipstick who chewed paan and spat it on the ground. It smelled just like the kotha I was in before but looked a lot bigger.

We walked down a corridor towards somewhere that smelt of chai and onions which made me very hungry. I remembered that the little bowl of rice was all I had eaten in days. My stomach growled like a little lion. I was scared the

Madame would hear it and be angry at me but she did not seem to notice. There were quite a few children around the corridor who seemed to be helping the ladies with the washing. They were all a lot smaller than me. I thought the Madame would stop and show me where I was to wash clothes but she did not. We kept walking and then went up some stairs. As we walked I kept waiting for her to show me where I was meant to work but we came to one of the rooms and she took me inside of it. I came in and there was a big, comfy looking bed with red sheets. There was also a little cassette player in the corner. I recognised it straight away because lots of the women in the other kotha had them and would play lots of songs from the new Bollywood films. One lady would play them over and over until all of the inside of the tape came falling out. I would sometimes sit outside the rooms where the music was coming from hoping to catch a few songs before the Madame came and shouted at me for not working.

Also in the room there was a wardrobe, a chair and a mirror. I looked around wondering why I had been brought here. The Madame bent down and spoke to me in Hindi, her voice sounding raspy like she smoked a lot. "Do you like this room?" she asked with the fake smile still on. I nodded my head, unsure why I had been shown it.

"This is your room now. Not for anyone else, only you.

And this," she said, walking to the wardrobe to reveal a brand new sari, "is yours. These clothes are dirty and old," she said pointing to me. "This will make you look so beautiful," she said, pulling it from the wardrobe and holding it for me to see. I looked at it with my mouth open as the light reflected off the sequins like it was a fish swimming in the water. It was more beautiful than any of the saris which the women were wearing downstairs. Red, blue and gold. I couldn't believe it. In all my time in the kothas I just had people's old clothes when they were worn out and full of holes. I looked at the Madame, waiting for her to laugh and tell me it was a joke but she just kept smiling and held it out for me to touch. I slowly held out my hand and felt how soft it was. I rubbed my hand over the sequins and giggled, excited by my present.

Maybe I was wrong and the Madame was actually really nice. She had given me such a big room. Was I allowed to sleep on the bed? I would have to ask her. Maybe there were other girls who would be sleeping in here that might be angry if I took the bed. She had said it was only for me but I had been made lots of promises that were broken as soon as they were spoken.

I wondered if Paravarti, Minu, Keva and Kareena had all been given their own rooms too. Maybe this place would be better than the other kothas. I hoped that I would see lots of Kareena, I wanted to make sure she was OK. Maybe life would be better here. Maybe all of us would be happy.

The Madame was still grinning, holding out the sari, and then she asked if I wanted to try it on. I nodded quickly, scared it would be taken away at any moment and she handed it to me. I laid it down on the bed then suddenly panicked. No one had ever been nice enough to give me a sari. I had never even wore one except on the roof with Sheila when we would just wrap them around ourselves and giggle, pretending to be film stars. I couldn't just wrap this one around me like a bed sheet in front of the Madame.

I stood quietly looking at it, thinking what to do. I was too embarrassed to tell her I had never worn one. For the first time that morning her smile fell off her face. She asked what was wrong and if I did not like the gift. I said I did but I would wear it later. The smile then came back and she offered to help me put it on, saying they were difficult to wear at first. I nodded, glad that she was so kind to help me.

Then I had another problem. The Madame stood waiting for me to get undressed to help me wear the sari, but I had never taken my clothes off in front of anyone. I woke up in my clothes, slept in my clothes and would run in to the showers quickly very early in the morning before anyone else was awake. I was too skinny and had grown a lot recently. Also my chest was beginning to grow and get lumpy, but it didn't look anything like any of the ladies in the films or the ladies I would sometimes see splashing water at each other in the shower block at the old kotha. They were beautiful but I was just bony and had knees which seemed to bend in.

I slowly began to undress, removing my old salwar kameez, but keeping my underwear on as I stood nervously covering myself with my arms. The Madame stood there and looked at my body as if she was studying a painting. Then she pulled out some new underwear from the wardrobe and threw them to me, asking me to put them on. I stood there, waiting for her to turn around but she just kept looking at me, nodding. I took them off quickly, trying to cover myself as I pulled on the new ones, tears burning my eyes. Even though it was a warm day I suddenly felt very cold. I did not like the way the Madame kept looking at me. While I was standing there she came up and moved my hands away from my body, making me turn around with my arms outstretched. She kept smiling and nodding, even as my face grew wet with tears.

After what seemed like forever she helped me to put the sari on. Now I just wanted to put my old clothes back on though. It felt strange and the sequins scratched my skin. Even though it was new I now felt dirty wearing it. She walked me over to the mirror and stood there smiling at my reflection. "You look beautiful," she said, her hands resting on my shoulders. Then she knelt down and clipped a silver anklet on me too, shaking it as she did. "See, beautiful," she repeated as it chimed. I looked up at my reflection but felt a long way from beautiful. The sari now looked silly, the light shining on the sequins looked like a broken mirror in the sunlight.

The Madame looked at my sad expression in the mirror, the tears drying on my cheeks. "I have given you this new sari, your own room and still you have this sad face! Maybe you don't deserve them. Maybe I will take them all and give them to someone else," she said, her voice getting louder as she became angrier. Then she stopped and took a deep breath. The smile came back to her face as if she had just breathed it in. "Never mind. It is a difficult day for you," she said more softly.

"Maybe some music will put a smile on that beautiful face of yours?" she said walking towards the cassette player and pressing play. A familiar voice came bursting out of it. I recognised it from one of the new Bollywood films which starred Aishwarya Rai. The song was beautiful and told of her love of her husband who had gone to war and she wished for him to return. It had always made me smile and wish that I could be in one of the films like this but today I did not want to smile. I still felt embarrassed at the way the Madame had looked at me.

She began to dance slowly to the music, moving her hands as if they were telling a story as she slowly began to take the sari off of her shoulder. I did not know what to do so I stared at the ground hoping that she would stop. She stopped the music and walked over to me, standing with her hands on her hips. "You have to watch. Tomorrow night you will be doing this by yourself to please a man who has paid a lot of money. A white man. A Gora. If he is not happy then neither am I or Dasji. Now, you watch me and afterwards you will copy."

I was scared and this time when the music started I tried to watch the Madame and remember what she did with her hands as she gracefully moved them around. After a minute or two she took the sari from her shoulder and let it fall to the ground as she ran her hands over her chest, all the time looking me in the eye and smiling. It looked very silly and I was embarrassed to see her doing this so I looked away again at the ground. I did not know how this was meant to please anyone. It made me want to run away so I do not know why anyone would pay money for someone to do this.

Immediately she stopped and walked over to me, this time though she slapped me hard across the cheek then pulled my face up towards her so that she could look into my eyes. "You must watch and learn. There are many things I must teach you before tomorrow. No more tears," she ordered, raising her hand again.

After that she started for a third time and I managed to watch until the very end, feeling sick as she danced. When she finished she looked at me and told me it was my turn to copy. I shook my head and looked at the ground, too scared to look up. Again she came and slapped me hard demanding I do it now. When I still said no she walked straight out of the room, slamming the door hard as she went. I hoped that was the end of it and they would just give me a job back in the kitchen and washing saris, even if it made my hands sore. I didn't mind sleeping on the floor in the kitchen. I would be very happy to leave this room and sari now and go back to life before.

After about ten minutes of sitting on the edge of the bed the door to the room burst open again. The Madame was there again but this time she was holding Kareena by one arm and a stick in the other. She threw her on the ground as they entered, Kareena screaming as she fell.

"This time you will do it," the Madame said, "or the little girl will be getting hit. Each time you stop or do it wrong she will be punished." She held up the stick and I jumped to my feet, Kareena looking at me with eyes that were huge and scared. As quick as I could I started moving my hands around like I was trying to button up an invisible shirt. Kareena continued to watch me, unsure of what I was doing.

"Slowly. Much more slowly," the Madame barked. "You are rushing around like a crazy cat. Be slow. Look at me and smile to show how happy you are." I tried to smile but it was very difficult to look happy when I felt like crying.

After forever the song stopped and I was wearing nothing but my under clothes and lying on the ground like the Madame had shown me. She nodded. Kareena was still staring at me with wide eyes holding her hands over her head for protection. The Madame clapped her hands and shouted "again!" as she rewound the tape for the same song.

I was made to practise many times until the Madame held up her hand to show that I had done enough. I grabbed my old clothes from the bed and put them back on, getting away from the sari as if it was a snake waiting to bite me if I was to put it back on. It almost felt like I could pretend that nothing had happened if I was back in my old clothes.

Over the next few hours the Madame taught me things to do which she said would please a man, raising the stick to Kareena anytime that I asked a question or said that I would not do something. These were horrible things which should not be talked about. I now knew exactly what had gone on in the other rooms in the kotha and felt sick that this was what the men had been paying to do when they came there.

As it got dark and noises were heard from downstairs the Madame said I was now ready and that everyone would be pleased tomorrow as she smiled at me again, that smile which she had earlier which was too wide to be believed. She spoke softly to me, saying I was now the jewel of the kotha and had to act like it and that if I did there would be many new saris and perfumes and sweets. I didn't want anything else from her though. I did not want this big room or the sari or the stupid cassette player. I just wanted to be back with my daddy in a place far away from here.

The Madame stood up and pointed with the stick to the door for Kareena to leave. She turned and looked at me one last time and I was unsure if anyone had ever looked so scared. She gave a small wave at me just before she left, then turned and I heard a small sob as she ran out of the door.

The Madame turned to me. "Yes, you will be very happy here and make me very happy. If not," she pointed with her stick to the door which Kareena had just left, "she will know about it."

She turned and left, leaving me alone in a room that was too big for me and was now full of horrible thoughts. I lay on the floor, not wanting to touch the bed, but did not sleep at all. I was too worried about what the next day was going to bring.

I stayed in the room all by myself the next day until the sunset. I had never been alone for more than an hour or so before as there was always someone around or a job which needed doing. Even if the people were loud and bossy it was better than being all alone with no-one at all to talk to. I wondered if this was how everyday would be and wished I could see Kareena and make sure she was OK. I would have to do everything I had been asked to keep her safe. So many days I had longed for music to listen to while I worked but now I sat in silence, the first beat of the music leaving me feeling unclean.

When it had become dark the Madame burst into my room carrying a small box, the silly smile still on her face. She sat and commanded that I go over to her as she pulled lots of make-up from the box. I had never worn it before and it felt strange having the Madame put it on my face. I kept blinking my eyes, scared the brush would hurt me which made the Madame angry. She made my cheeks red and put green around my eyes which she said was to make me look more beautiful. Then she combed my hair, after helping me dress in the sari. "So beautiful," she said shaking her head. She brought me in front of the mirror but I did not even recognise myself with my dark eyes and red lips. My face felt itchy under the makeup but I did not dare to touch it. It was like my face now belonged to someone else.

The Madame left then returned with the fat man a few minutes later. He smiled and ran a chubby hand through my hair. "Very nice," he said, "she is ready."

The Madame nodded and disappeared once more. The fat man sat down in the chair, pulling it around so it sat in front of the bed. I was worried it might break as it creaked under his weight and wished it would. He pulled out a cigar and lit it, filling the room with the smell of heavy smoke, all of the time looking at me. "This will be your first time so I am here to make sure things go well," he said. "You don't need to be scared when your Uncle Das is here. I will look after you," he said, licking his lips and blowing out smoke.

I wanted to say it was him who was making me scared but knew it would be a silly thing to do. I tried to smile but my stomach was feeling twisted and almost as if it was alive and moving around.

"Remember," he said, "there are nice prizes for good girls who work well, but bad things for those who don't. This man has paid very good money for you and you will be having to make sure he gets his money worth so that he comes back again with his friends. He is a gora, white man. Who knows, if you please him he may buy you a castle," he said laughing. "After him I wish to introduce you to a dear friend of mine, Superintendent Roy."

I was worried, wondering why he would be friends with the police. In the last kotha the Madame had always been scared of the police and if they ever came into the building there was a special room below the building all of the children had to hide in so that we did not get in trouble for being there. We were told stories by the Madame about children who had been found in kothas and had been locked up in prison for the rest of their lives so we were very sure not to make any noise or even sneeze. We hid quite a few times but we were very good at hiding and never got found. Why would police be invited here? Was I to be arrested for being too young and living here in the kotha? I did not want to go to jail forever.

At that moment I heard the Madame outside the door speaking in English. I had been taught English by my daddy when I was little but it sounded very strange hearing the Madame speaking it. Sometimes the goras who visited the kotha would speak English but I would always pretend that I did not understand so that I would not have to speak to them.

As the door began to slowly open Das pointed at me to turn on the cassette player. I heard the door close behind the gora as he came into the room. As the first beat of the song began I tried to remember all that the Madame had taught me and I slowly began to turn around, my hands moulded like a swan's beak. I closed my eyes getting ready for all that was about to happen.

# Chapter Twenty Nine

I was still stunned as Das leaned over, his hot breath touching my face as he untied the rope binding me to the table. I stood unsteadily, surveying the scene before me. Roy's body lay splayed on the floor, outlined with blood. Tom's corpse lay on the table and Das was bent over, tossing the money and drugs into the sports bag, the gun tucked into his belt. The two bodies served as a reminder of what was soon to happen to me if I could not get Das the promised money. I was also not so naive as to realise that this would be my fate even if I somehow miraculously found him more cash, which was an impossibility as that had been our only remaining account. The end of my existence on earth had been miraculously postponed, but was soon to expire.

Das stood up, threw the bag over his shoulder and held the gun on me. "I will give you one hour to be finding me the money. If fail you will die. If you try to run, you will die. If you do anything to make people notice me, you will die. You will be doing very well just to be staying alive. Do not think just because we are in the street I will not shoot you like a dog. I will. Now come, we must hurry," he said motioning with the gun for me to lead the way up the stairs. He kept the gun trained on my back and walked quickly behind, stopping only to spit over his shoulder in the direction of Roy.

As we reached the top of the stairs I unlocked the metal door with the key which Das handed me. Once the key had clicked in the lock the door suddenly flew inwards, knocking me backwards into Das who dropped the sports bag, sending a flutter of money across the floor, the notes sliding in the blood and dirt. Six Policemen burst into the room, rifles all locked on Das as they circled him like a dangerous animal in the wild. Before anyone could speak he had grabbed me tightly around the neck holding his gun to my skull. He spun me around, shouting loudly in Hindi at each man, challenging them to shoot. I felt like he would choke me soon even if he wasn't panicked enough to pull the trigger on me.

After a long tirade Das fell silent and no-one in the police attempted to speak, a stand-off ensuing until another figure stepped around the door. He was dressed in a faded blue shirt, had wild white hair and glasses held together with a plaster. He stood, arms folded and then broke the silence, "Das. It's over. Put the gun down," he said in perfect English, with a great deal of self-assurance. Das suddenly looked even more irate at this entrance.

"You!" he said, the gun shaking with fury. "You should have died a long time ago Dalit scum! This time I will be making sure of it!" he said, extending his arm.

Two shots rang out within split seconds of each other. I fell to the ground as I was released from the vice like grip of

Das, holding my ears as they rung like church bells. The world had fallen into silence and I could see the police all running, mouths wide as they shouted instructions to one another. One ran over to me, kneeling at my side.

I looked down and saw that the front of my top was splattered with blood. I lay my hand on it, and pulled away a wet sticky handprint. The Policeman was shouting something at me but in my world of silence this meant nothing. I put the hand back, feeling for a wound, adrenaline pumping round my body. I frantically groped around feeling nothing, breathing a huge sigh of relief as the policeman pointed behind me to Das who was now being held on the ground by three men, rifles held to his head. His right hand was missing two fingers, blood spurting down his back as one of the Police struggled to grip his arms to put him in handcuffs.

Looking up, the man who had spoken to Das was clutching the top of his arm, a trickle of blood escaping from between his fingers as he stared forlornly at the body of Tom on the table. His melancholy was momentarily halted though as one of the other officers walked over, revealing the contents of the sports bag to him. He smiled grimly and with a nod of satisfaction he motioned for the Officers to take Das away. Despite his injury he still struggled and fought with the officers before being hoisted up the stairs, four rifles poking him begrudgingly into submission. Another Officer walked behind them, staggering slightly at the weight of the sports bag slung over his shoulder. As he disappeared through the door I wondered briefly if I would get my savings back but that seemed inconsequential after all that had just happened.

The sixth Officer milled around looking at the two bodies and speaking hurriedly into his mobile phone as the man in the faded blue shirt tied a strip of cloth around his wound and walked towards me. His face was heavily lined with worry but warm and open, offering reassurance like a warm mug of soup after the unsettling events that I had encountered in the last few hours. Almost as if he knew me he came and squatted next to me on the floor, tentatively putting a hand on my shoulder. His eyes were bright and alert, a sense of triumph mingled with sorrow swirled in them, together but separate, like oil mixed in a pool of water. I could see this was a man who understood my grief and confusion and for the first time since my arrival in India I felt like I would be safe. I looked into his face then subconsciously nestled my head in his shirt, tears falling as I released all of the pain and fear which had almost destroyed me today. He sat, gently patting me on the back as my tears fell with reckless abandon, soaking his front. Eventually I stopped, pulling back as I became more self-conscious, the tears subsiding. He offered me a comforting smile which I returned, smearing the tears across my face with my palm. He pulled a handkerchief from his pocket and offered it to me, which I gladly took.

My ears still tingled, but I was able to hear as he soothingly placed his hands on both my shoulders and whispered, "it's OK, it's all over now. You need not fear. You are safe with us."

I looked around and saw that the place was again swarming with Police in protective clothing taking photos of Roy and Tom and furiously scribbling notes.

"We are not all the same as Superintendent Roy," he said in recognition of the suspicion in my eyes as I observed their activity. "I am so sorry for all you have been through Mrs Parker."

"Rachel," I said quickly, shuddering at the way my own name made my skin prickle after the way it had dripped from the lips of Roy. "Please, just call me Rachel."

He nodded then seemed to falter, looking for the correct words to say. "Rachel, I am so sorry for what happened to your husband. He was a very good, kind man."

I snorted, my confusion and rage at Tom rising again. "If you call someone who sells children to prostitution a good and kind man. Someone who sells drugs and murders people a good and kind man, then yeah. In fact, he should be made a saint!" I said sarcastically, my voice rising until I saw the hurt on his face. "I'm sorry, I didn't need to say that. I know you were only trying to be nice. You wouldn't have known all that he was involved with. The kind of man he really was," I said apologetically.

"Rachel, I knew Tom well. Very well. In fact, he was the most courageous man I ever met." He paused and looked at the ground as I sat puzzled, trying to figure out what this meant. "I am very sorry to say, if it was not for me, your husband would still be alive. If anyone is culpable for all this, the blame lies solely with me," he said, not meeting me with his eyes.

"What? Who are you? What did you do to him?" I asked, defensively, drawing my arms and legs in to distance myself from him, not ready for another disturbing surprise.

He sighed deeply. "Who I am and who I was are very different I am afraid. I was known by your husband as Superintendent Anthony Dipal." He reached inside his pocket and pulled out an envelope which had my name scrawled across it in Tom's handwriting with three kisses below it. "I could explain but I think that is best left for your husband."

He handed me the letter which I took in stunned silence, then he stood and looked at me. "I will be just there," he said motioning to the steps, "if you want to talk once you have read it. Again, I am so sorry."

I watched as he trudged over to the steps, head hung in defeat after he had glanced once more at the body of Tom. I watched him until he was seated and then turned my attention to the mysterious envelope. I turned it over silently, feeling its weight in my hands. I ran my fingers over each letter of my name, intrigued and anxious about its contents. I touched it like an alien object, unsure of what it may do, trying to summon the courage to see what it may contain. After a brief moment, curiosity besieged me. I relented and carefully prised open the letter, scanning the lines eagerly for some sort of clue that would make all these events become clearer. His first words chilled my blood;

*Dear Rachel,*
*Everything I have told you is untrue...*

I paused, taking a moment to breathe deeply, knowing that the following pages were set to once more destroy the illusions I had of who my husband was. I just hoped that what was written would be true and allow me to somehow lay him to rest in my heart.

I continued onwards with the letter, gripped by every word of his confession as I rode an emotional rollercoaster, in part feeling bitterness and resentment, part sorrow and rage on his behalf and also a deep pity and love for the courage of the husband I had lost. Once finished I sat numb once more, unsure how to process all that I had been told by Tom from beyond the grave. He had a child! A daughter. Never once had he spoken to me of her existence! I could not begin to imagine what he had been through, why had he not found it in his heart to open up and share all this hurt and pain with me.

I stood and walked through the bustle of police officers, coming once more to my husband's body. Once there, I looked at his face and felt as if I was truly seeing him for the first time. I ran my fingers over the lines on his face, feeling his sorrow and despair and wished that I could have shared in this whole secret part of his life, if not to help to at least understand.

Bitterness burned in my heart but was extinguished by a wave of pity and regret for all that we had both lost. He had suffered so much too. I reached down and took his hand, gently prying open his stiff fingers and removing my wedding ring. Then I slipped it once more onto my finger, lifted his hand and kissed it before gently placing it back at his side. I once more felt the indented skin on his wedding finger and went to the still warm body of Roy to retrieve Tom's ring. Holding my breath I uncurled his slender fingers, the ring slipping straight off. I glanced up at his face, now lifeless, yet his lip still curled in a cruel snarl. I carefully backed away, being sure not to get any of his blood on my shoes.

After cleaning the ring on my top I placed it back on Tom's finger, then lay my hand on his, a thousand words, questions, statements I wanted to say raging in my mind, but I simply leaned forward and into his ear I whispered, "I forgive you. I love you."

I remained there a moment, a peace settling in my heart before I walked slowly over to Dipal who was cleaning his glasses on his shirt. He looked up at me nervously and I looked back, offering a sad smile of understanding to which he nodded. I sat next to him on the concrete step and looking at the ground I asked the one thing I still needed from him, "please, tell me how Tom died."

## Chapter Thirty

Even though I had my eyes closed I knew that the fat man and the gora were sitting there watching me, thinking about things which the Madame had told me last night. I wanted to run far away from here but knew that Kareena would be hurt if I ever tried to. Instead I closed my eyes and thought about the music and what I had been told to do. The voice singing the music became higher and higher and I began to stamp my feet on the ground to make a tingling sound from the bells on my anklet.

I opened my eyes to see both men seated and watching me grinning. They were sharing a cigarette that smelled very strong and funny and both of them had red eyes like bad men in the films. I kept dancing and decided to look at the ground because their faces made me want to cry. I began to turn around on the spot, and touched the edge of my sari, ready to take it off as the Madame had shown me, but my cheeks went hot and I couldn't do it so I kept waving my hands and stamping my feet. After a minute or so the fat man began to stop smiling.

"Take it off," he ordered me in Hindi, smacking his cane on the ground. "We did not pay good money just to see you dancing. We could pay less to see far better dancers. Quickly, quickly. Roy will be here soon too and you must perform for him also," he said, clapping his hands together at me like I was a small dog. Slowly I turned around and took the sari material in my hand. The gora had eyes that looked far away as he sat with a little bit of spit at the side of his smiling mouth while he clapped to the beat of the music.

I closed my eyes, counting in my head until all of this was over, knowing that it could not last forever. I slowly took the sari off my shoulder and held it in my left hand so that my petticoat was uncovered.

"Good, good," urged the fat man while the gora sat there giggling like he was stupid. It was too much. I really wanted to run. To tell them that I was not going to do this but then I thought again of Kareena and her huge eyes looking at me for help. I breathed deeply and prepared to keep going. I was sure that by the time I counted to one hundred it would all be finished. If not I would have to start again from one. I took the sari and began to unwind it around myself as both men stared at me.

Suddenly the door flew open and I screamed, jumping backward and pulling my sari over my chest. Standing in the doorway was a short man with white hair that went everywhere and a pair of glasses. Around his neck was a big camera and in his hand was a gun. Standing behind him was a gora who had his arm around the Madame and a gun pointed at her head as he pushed her through the door. He had wild eyes which moved quickly from side to side and then stopped on me as I threw myself against the far wall to try and hide.

As we looked at each other his face suddenly went from being mean and angry to very happy. A huge grin touched both sides of his face and tears began coming out of his eyes. Many times I had been taken away and I wondered if that was why he was here with the guns. I wondered if he was going to hurt me but he looked too happy to do that. Then he did something which shocked me so much. He put the gun away and ran over to me shouting my old name, 'Aisha! Aisha!' over and over again and kissed me on the forehead as I sat in the corner. I was frightened and didn't know how he knew my name. Then he gently put his hand under my chin and lifted my head so that I could look into his sparkly, wet eyes.

"Aisha. It's me. I'm your dad! It's time to come home my little Princess."

I sat, my mouth open, not sure what to say. I had some memories of my daddy when I was very small but I had not seen him in so long. Now he had come to save me! I too began to cry and wrapped my arms around his neck like I had wanted to do for so many years. So many nights I had cried myself to sleep hoping he would come. Could I leave this horrible kotha with him now? Did I have to keep dancing?

He gripped me tightly as if he thought I was going to run away and he kept saying my name over and over. I had so many questions I wanted to ask him! So many things I wanted to tell him. I couldn't believe it was really him.

He let me go, then pulled out of his pocket a photo which was old and had many creases in it. He held it up so I could see it.

"This is the last photo I ever had of you," he said, his voice shaking. "I've never stopped looking for you. I didn't even know if you were still alive!"

Again he hugged me, until the sound of a gun rang out, making us both jump.

We looked across the room and the man with daddy was holding his gun above his head as it smoked. The Madame, the fat man and the gora were all kneeling on the ground. Daddy's friend was shouting at the fat man to pass his gun along the floor to him which he did while swearing under his breath about him being a dirty Dalit. The gora looked very frightened and still had spit coming out of his mouth while the Madame was looking at me with her eyes narrowed. Daddy leant over and kissed me on the top of the head then stood up taking the gun out of his belt. I wanted to tell him to stop but he had walked across the room before I had the chance. He pulled something to make his gun click then held it in the fat man's fat face. When daddy had his gun out, his friend began taking pictures of the room. He photographed the three of them on their knees and also me next to the bed after he had let me pull my sari back on properly. He then took one of daddy as he stood with his gun on the man's head. It was a fancy camera and the picture came out of the bottom straight away. He pulled it out and then walked over to try and calm daddy who was shouting loudly at the man.

Daddy was screaming about him taking me away from him and how he was going to get his revenge. His friend put a hand on his shoulder and whispered something in his ear too quietly for me to hear. Daddy turned and looked at me, his hand still shaking. He stayed still like a statue for a long time, with the gun still in the fat man's face, then slowly began to bring it down. When he had moved the gun the fat man growled at him, "you can take her, dirty whore." In a second daddy brought the gun down hard on his head, knocking him to the floor, his belly spread out under him like a whale. I thought daddy was then going to shoot him but instead he lent down and felt his neck, then said that he was alive to his friend.

Daddy stood and held his hand out to me, saying that we had to leave straight away. It was only then that I noticed all of the voices and shouting in the corridor. He took my hand tightly and I squeezed it back so that I wouldn't lose him again like that day at the market. I never wanted that to happen again. He had found me and I would never let go.

We ran out of the door, daddy and his friend both holding their guns in the air as we stepped on to the corridor which was now full with the women in their bright saris and also the three men who had taken me and the other girls out of the basement the other day. People were shouting and pushing to get a better view but everyone stepped back as the guns were waved, leaving a gap for us to pass through.

We ran quickly down the corridor, scared that someone might try to stop us, but no one did and we were soon down the stairs, daddy's friend taking pictures as we ran of all of the girls in the kotha. As we got halfway down the stairs though I saw a pair of eyes looking at me from between the legs of two screaming women. Kareena. I reached out a hand and she took it and joined our little gang as we ran to the front door, to a new life, to freedom. She giggled nervously as she ran along, her hand feeling so small compared to Daddy's which was still tightly squeezing my other hand and pulling me forward.

In a second we burst out of the door which I had been pushed through only two nights ago, the image of the Madame hitting other girls as they struggled off the truck still in my head. That night was silent apart from the Madame's shouting and the sound of her hand on the girl's bare skin. Tonight though there was so much noise, but the shouts and cries of the people in the kotha faded as we ran around a corner, our feet slapping the pavement and our deep breathing becoming the only noise as the kotha disappeared from sight.

I allowed myself to grin as we ran; my daddy had come to rescue me. We could be a family again. Maybe Kareena could be my sister. I always wanted to have a little sister. I would never have to dance like that again for those horrible, red eyed men. I was safe. Every step we took from the kotha, the fat man and the Madame, the more I smiled and felt like everything was going to be OK.

As we turned another corner I could feel Kareena's hand slipping from mine. I turned and looked and could see her face was bright red, her little legs going so fast but still not keeping up with us as her bare feet moved along the concrete. Her eyes again were pleading with me to slow down, small tears escaping her cheeks. I shouted daddy and he turned, seeing Kareena for the first time, a surprised look on his face. He stopped and quickly bent down, putting a hand on my face and smiling gently at Kareena.

"We are not safe yet," he said, breathing deeply as he spoke, making it difficult to understand as he spoke in English, a language I had hardly heard since I had been taken from him. "We have to keep running. But soon, soon we will be safe. Together again. Forever this time," he said kissing me on the forehead and standing to run again.

Kareena looked at me puzzled, not really understanding any of what was going on. I suddenly realised she would not understand the English. "Baba," I said to her, pointing to daddy. She burst into a big smile, but before she could speak we were being pulled along again, into a smaller street. A moment later I heard angry shouting and gun fire once more as the big black car which the fat man travelled in really quickly sped past the street we were in, but luckily he did not see us as daddy had pulled us into a doorway to hide. He pressed a finger to the lips of Kareena and me as a group of men also ran past the entrance to our road, shouting loudly in Hindi.

We waited a moment till it was quiet again then slowly got up, daddy's friend pulling out his keys and opening the door to a car on the street. He motioned with his hand to get in the car and I looked at Daddy to make sure he was coming too. He nodded, and smiled. I took Kareena's hand and we climbed in, daddy's friend starting the car engine.

Then a voice behind daddy screamed at him. He turned around and there stood a man in a policeman's uniform who had a long, sharp nose which made him look a bit like a rat. In his mouth was a cigarette which was making his whole face glow red like a demon. In his hand he held a gun which was pointed at daddy's chest as he walked towards us. I banged on the window and screamed at daddy to get in the car. He looked at me through the window one last time and then I heard the crack of the gun and saw him fall to the ground.

The car was already moving as I tried to jump out, daddy's

friend holding me in by the arm as we pulled away, the policeman firing shots at us until we were around the corner.

As soon as he had arrived, daddy was gone.

## Chapter Thirty One

Dipal finished relaying the events from outside the brothel, stopping at the moment he had driven away, leaving Tom in the street with Roy firing at the car. After this he stopped, placing his head in his hands, his fingers sliding into his wild hair. "I shouldn't have left him there to die like a stray dog in the street. I shouldn't have done that." He pulled his head up to face me, his eyes fixed on mine. "Please Rachel, I ask for your forgiveness. I should have fought. I should have at least stayed to rescue his body. I owed him that much," he stated solemnly. I placed my hand on his.

"Please, you have done more than enough. From what Tom says in here," I said, raising the letter, "you have been the only one who truly stood by him through this awful time in his life. I need to thank you, not forgive you. All the sacrifices you have made." He shrugged ruefully and looked at the ground.

"Rachel, there is one final thing which I need to tell you. After Tom was killed..." he began, but was halted in his speech as a police officer adorned with stripes marched over to us. Dipal stood to attention, subliminally straightening his shirt. The officer looked at me and nodded politely.

"Rachel, may I introduce you to Chief Commissioner Pavarmani," he said officially, helping me to my feet as he spoke. The Commissioner held out his weathered hand for me to shake.

"Mrs Parker, I am most sorry for your loss. I assure you we are doing all that is most possible in our power to bring justice for your husband," he said gravely.

I nodded courteously before he turned his attention to Dipal.

"You are responsible for all of this," he said, motioning with his hand to the room, the bodies and the numerous police officers. "You were not under authority of the Police but took it upon yourself to do all this. What do you have to say for yourself?" he barked. Dipal opened his mouth to respond but closed it again, shrugging apologetically.

"Nothing. You have nothing to say? Even after working alone and taking photographs of a kotha to have the most wanted criminal in India arrested, you have nothing to say? This story will be all over the papers tomorrow, showing our diligent work against these criminals and how we have been victorious." The Chief Commissioner's face grew less stern as he held out his hand to a stunned Dipal. "We need you to be coming back. You can begin first thing on the Monday." He heartily shook Dipal's hand, nodded at me once more and was gone into the crowd of brown shirts.

I placed a hand on Dipal's arm and smiled. "Well done. After your tireless work, you deserve it."

"There are more important things to discuss than this," he said, waving his hand dismissively. "Das has been responsible for so much pain and suffering, in your life and the life of so many others. It is only a small step but I hope that his arrest will bring freedom to some." He pushed the glasses back up his nose and stared at me intently. "There is one more thing which I must do to try and alleviate some of this suffering." He turned and shouted an order in Hindi to one of the officers waiting by the door. After a moment he returned with his hands on the shoulder of two girls, one about ten years old with a round face and pig tails and the other a little older with amazing emerald eyes, both of them looking only at the ground as they entered.

"Rachel, this is Kareena and Aisha. They will be needing someone to look after them," he said as the two girls turned their expectant eyes up towards me.

*While the story of Scar Tissue is purely fictional, the issues raised are all too real. The charities listed below are all close to my heart; they fight to tackle the issues of human trafficking and/or caste inequality. Please visit their websites to discover more about the great work they are doing.*

*David Skivington*

## Life Association

My wife and I are currently working for a charity called *Life Association* in Andhra Pradesh, India. We are teaching in one of their orphanage schools which provide a home and education for children born as Dalits. They have a number of other projects which all work with those from the Dalit caste, who often face immense persecution. One of these projects works in the Dharavi slum in Mumbai with potters who create stunningly beautiful candles and holders as well as producing a range of Indian spices (which make amazing presents!) You can find out more at **www.lifeassociation.org.uk**.

## Dalit Freedom Network

Dalit Freedom Network UK is a human rights / development charity working to end human trafficking and slavery of India's Dalits (Untouchables). Around half of all those in modern slavery globally are Dalits in India. DFN UK raises awareness and engages in advocacy in the UK to pressure for change in India. They also support on-the-ground anti-trafficking and development projects in India, including schools (100+), healthcare, economic development and women's empowerment programmes, refuge shelters and trafficking prevention. DFN UK invites people of goodwill to support their work through raising awareness, lobbying or fundraising. End Dalit Trafficking: Prevention Through Education.
Find out more at **www.dfn.org.uk**.

## Nvader

Nvader is an international human rights organization with offices in New Zealand and South East Asia. The mission of Nvader is to RESCUE victims of sex trafficking by gathering evidence of specific cases, facilitate the PROSECUTION of the perpetrators responsible and bring down the criminal networks involved. They inspire, engage and EMPOWER local communities to effectively combat this modern form of slavery. You can learn more about their work at **www.nvader.org**.

## Hope for Justice

Hope for Justice is an anti-human trafficking organisation rescuing and assisting victims of modern-day slavery in the UK. HFJ specialist investigators work closely with the police to build bridges of trust with victims who may be too afraid to cooperate with the authorities. Their team removes them from their situations of devastating exploitation and they support the prosecution of traffickers as well as campaigning to protect victims.
Visit **www.hopeforjustice.org.uk**.

## Stop the Traffik

STOP THE TRAFFIK is a global movement of individuals, communities and organisations fighting to prevent human trafficking around the world. Every instance of trafficking involves a person being trafficked from a community into a community. Therefore the community must work together to prevent it. The organization work to inspire, inform, equip and mobilise communities to know what trafficking is and how to identify it; know how to protect themselves and others; know how to respond. Look on thier website to find out about their campaigns for change and how you can get involved.
Visit **www.stopthetraffik.org**